Hawaiian Hottie

I stopped short to gaze up at Lee. His big, gentle eyes held mine, as the moonlight danced off his jet black hair.

Lee stopped, too. "Have you ever surfed?"

I didn't want to lose favor with Lee, so I opted for honest-cute. "Does channel or Web surfing count?"

He threw his head back and laughed. "You're adorable, Cher. And sweet. Tell your boyfriend he's lucky to have you."

I couldn't believe it. Lee was fishing to find out if I had a hottie stashed away. I set him straight. "I don't have a boyfriend, Lee. But does your girlfriend know how poetic you are?" Like, you didn't have to get wet to fish.

Lee softly cupped my chin in his hand. Gently, he tilted my face up toward his. Just before our lips met, he murmured, "I don't have a girlfriend, Cher."

Clueless™ Books

CLUELESS™ • A novel by H. B. Gilmour based on the film written and directed by Amy Heckerling

CHER'S GUIDE TO . . . WHATEVER • H. B. Gilmour

CHER NEGOTIATES NEW YORK • Jennifer Baker

AN AMERICAN BETTY IN PARIS • Randi Reisfeld

ACHIEVING PERSONAL PERFECTION • H. B. Gilmour

CHER'S FURIOUSLY FIT WORKOUT • Randi Reisfeld

FRIEND OR FAUX • H. B. Gilmour

CHER GOES ENVIRO-MENTAL • Randi Reisfeld

BALDWIN FROM ANOTHER PLANET • H. B. Gilmour

TOO HOTTIE TO HANDLE • Randi Reisfeld

CHER AND CHER ALIKE • H. B. Gilmour

TRUE BLUE HAWAII • Randi Reisfeld

Available from ARCHWAY Paperbacks

For orders other than by individual consumers, Pocket Books grants a discount on the purchase of **10 or more** copies of single titles for special markets or premium use. For further details, please write to the Vice-President of Special Markets, Pocket Books, 1633 Broadway, New York, NY 10019-6785, 8th Floor.

For information on how individual consumers can place orders, please write to Mail Order Department, Simon & Schuster Inc., 200 Old Tappan Road, Old Tappan, NJ 07675.

Clueless™

True Blue Hawaii

Randi Reisfeld

AN ARCHWAY PAPERBACK
Published by POCKET BOOKS
New York London Toronto Sydney Tokyo Singapore

AN ARCHWAY PAPERBACK *Original*

An Archway Paperback published by
POCKET BOOKS, a division of Simon & Schuster Inc.
1230 Avenue of the Americas, New York, NY 10020

ISBN: 0-671-01162-6

First Archway Paperback printing September 1997

10 9 8 7 6 5 4 3 2 1

Printed in the U.S.A.

IL: 7+

Acknowledgments

The author sends a sincere "Mahalo" to everyone who helped and inspired! Fran Lebowitz, Anne Greenberg, Amira Rubin, and Paul Ruditis for coming up with the title, and especially Denis and Jane Kalfus for their off-the-beaten-track real-life adventures in Moo-ie—that is, Maui.

With love to Marvin, Scott, and Stefanie, awash in the spirit of aloha, always.

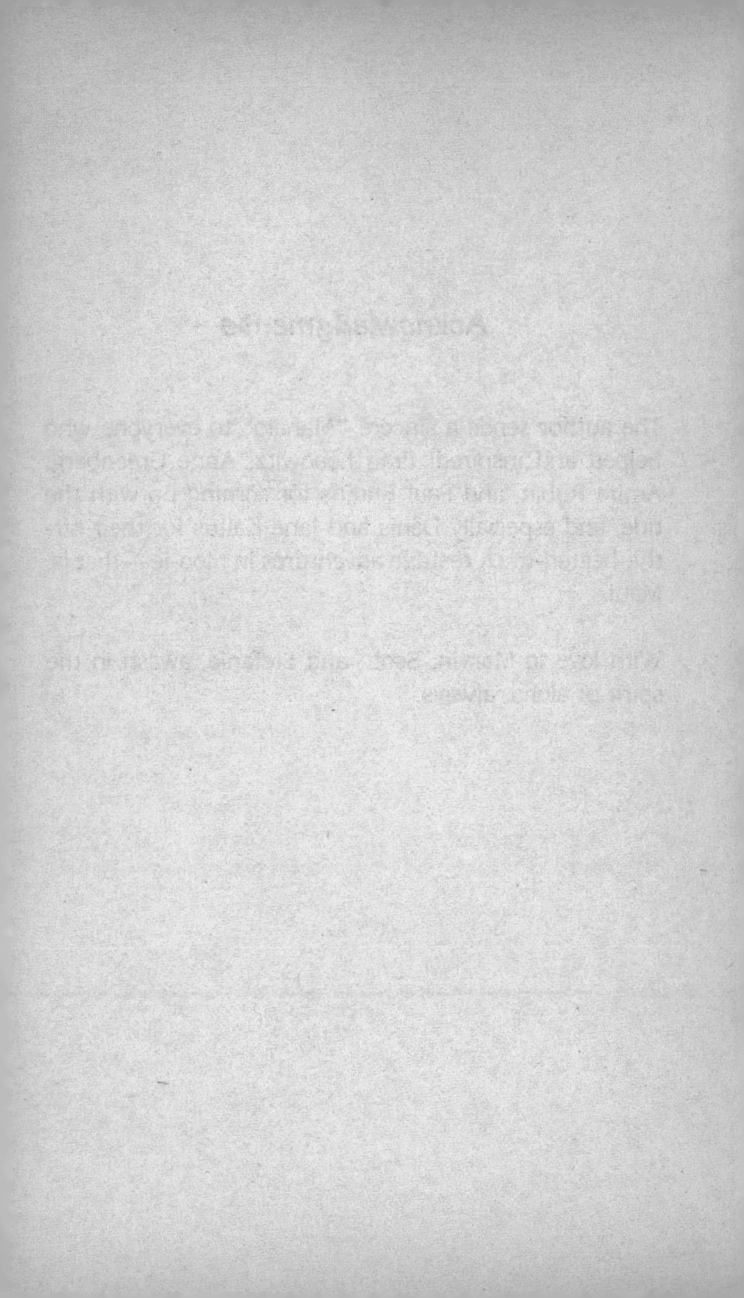

True Blue
Hawaii

Chapter 1

"The cranberry is kickin'!" my friend Murray exclaimed as he waved the new BMW catalog around for one and all to appreciate.

"Excuse me, creamy boysenberry is the cutting edge hue du jour," Amber, my crankiest friend, contradicted, waving her own catalog in Murray's face.

"Dudes! Exit the orchard—we're talking wheels, not toasted oats. Screaming, in-your-face yellow is what's happening on the street." New county heard from: Jesse Fiegenhut, who trades cars the way most people in our crowd trade one-ups, was furiously insistent on having the final say.

"Besides," he added, proffering a glossier, thicker catalog than either Murray or Amber had, "we're over the whole Beemers concept. This year's slammin' model T is the Humvee, boys and girls. It's high profile, high mobility, and has a higher purpose."

"Hello? The Humvee?" Amber snorted derisively. "That barely housebroken military vehicle? And remind me again, what exactly *is* its higher purpose? Besides being the ultimate accessory to an urban-guerrilla fashion ensemble?" Amber chortled at her bon mots. But she who chortles most, chortles alone.

Sean, who is Murray's ultimate friend accessory, leaned across the aisle to sneer at Jesse, "Yeah, what she said. And who elected you arbiter of everything automotive?" Sean, too, had been eyeballing a shiny new car brochure.

I leaned forward in my third-row seat and tried to concentrate on what Miss Geist, our social studies teacher, was saying. It's not that I don't care about the new car catalogs—hello, my Jeep is like totally ready for an overhaul—but sometimes Miss Geist has furiously fascinating tidbits to impart. And no matter what the topic is, she's always hyper-impassioned, a trait I fully applaud. I just wish she'd channel a little of that energy into her wardrobe.

Miss Geist was holding up a graphic of a fuzzy round baby birdlet and going, ". . . endangered species, like this California condor chick, and others, like the humpback whale, are defined as any that are threatened with extinction."

Then she proffered a long list. "Anyone can nominate an animal for the Official Endangered Species list, as long as they also present information for scientists to review about why it's endangered."

I regarded Miss Geist's outfit and decided to

nominate it for extinction. The blouse was a baby-rose lace-collared frilly confection. She'd paired it with a floral-patterned pleated skirt and opted for a tunic over both. It reminded me of that famous poem "An outfit divided against itself cannot prevail."

"Cher, did you have something to add?" Miss Geist, realizing I was the only one paying attention, sought my support.

I didn't want to let her down, so I did my best on short notice. "I was just wondering, um, why the plight of the baby condors and other endangered species isn't more publicized? I mean, animal-rights activists are way headline newsy these days. Like, aren't they always disrupting fashion shows and getting dragged away in handcuffs? The public sympathy vote should be in the bag."

Geist agreed and went off on a publicity tangent. I went back to surveying our classroom.

I go to Bronson Alcott High School, which is conveniently located in our Beverly Hills neighborhood, situated midway between the designer boutiques on Rodeo Drive and several upscale malls, all of which our students typically frequent. Today being like any other normal school day, my peer group was engaged in all our typical activities.

Cellular phones and beepers were in full melodious effect. A troika of Bettys named Janet, Summer, and Annabelle were in the back of the classroom, demonstrating new makeup techniques and ardently debating the new Bobbi Brown hues versus the new M.A.C. shades. A smattering of singletons, including class president Brian, science dweeb Ringo, and my alterna-friend Baez, were working intensely in their PowerBooks, sending E-mail to their cohorts in distant corners of the school. Our token slacker, Jackson, was napping; Ariel was experimenting on Jasmine's hair with the new Uncurl; and our Iranian contingent was arguing in Farsi.

Of course, since it was the day the new car catalogs came out, which the Beverly Hills dealerships had graciously delivered to all our lockers, several of my A-list fabulons were checking out the various models. It's the only time of the year that word doesn't have the prefix *super* attached to it.

We were all present and accounted for, with the glaring exception of my main t.b.—as in true blue friend—Dionne. She still hadn't debuted in school this morning and already it was third period. She'd beeped me earlier to say she'd be detained, and I made her apologies to Miss Geist, who might otherwise have felt insulted by De's tardy.

I checked my Movado and realized we were practically ready for our second commercial break. If De didn't show up soon, she'd be dancing on the precipice of missing her third class of the day. I decided to give her a buzz. Maybe she needed me.

I was wearing my StarTAC cellular in lieu of a pendant, so in one efficient motion I was able to speed dial her without taking my eyes off Miss Geist and her lecture. But all I got was the voice mail about De being on another line and would I care to forward my message to her mailbox. But when I pressed 3 for that option, I was informed by the guy whose voice is more annoying than the AOL "You've Got Mail" guy that De's mailbox was full. There was no room for my message.

I glanced over at Murray, De's up-through-and-including-high-school boyfriend. He'd just tossed the car catalog aside and flipped his own cellular closed.

"Paging De?" I guessed.

"No answer," he replied. "What's up with her, Cher? What's with the incommunicado thing?"

I shrugged my shoulders. If Murray didn't know, it meant he and De weren't frosted today. Their relationship has had as many ups and downs as the elevator at the Beverly Center. But my t.b. ESPN told me that De wasn't purposely dodging either Murray's calls or mine. She was probably just rampantly preoccupied with something else.

De and I are poly-fashionable icons here at school, student leaders in all things sartorial and trend enhanced. We enjoy the fervid adoration and fawning attention of all our worshippers, students and faculty alike. We take our responsibility as role models fully seriously. It's our credo to use our popularity for good causes, like the environment, transfer students, and all creatures large and small.

As if she could read my mind, Amber tapped me on the shoulder. "Where's your wittier half, Cher? Gone for another body-sculpting session? Or was there a sale at Gucci she couldn't resist?"

Leave it to Amber to project. That's where she would have been. Despite her vast financial resources and easy access to a poly-glut of personal shoppers, trainers, and aromatherapists, Amber Salk was terminally clueless: our group's foremost fashion victim.

Today she was in a leopard-print stretch turtleneck top and tiger-patterned skirt, an outfit screaming for inclusion on Miss Geist's condemned list.

"Wherever she is, Amber," I retorted, "when De does show up, at least her hair will represent a style from this millennium. Unlike yours . . . or are those ear muffs punctuating the sides of your head?"

Amber had aimed for the Princess Leia, but those two huge side buns made her look more like Igloo Me Amber. She shot me a W sign for "Whatever" and transferred her notoriously short attention span back to the Beemer catalog.

"For your term papers," Miss Geist was announcing, valiantly moving forward with her lesson, "each of you will be assigned one endangered animal to report on. You may do any sort of presentation you'd like: multimedia, sculpture, performance art, a video, a skit. This is my most creative class, so I'm expecting exciting presentations. Now—"

She consulted her Official Endangered Species list and cleared her throat. "Who wants the whooping crane?"

No one volunteered. Geist craned her neck and picked the first person she made eye contact with. "Sean? How about you? Would you like the whooping crane?"

Sean, attention-deficient as usual, was flummoxed. "The whooping crane? I think I already had that disease. I'm pretty sure I've been inoculated."

As Geist proceeded to inject Sean and the rest of the class with their assignments, I checked my watch again. Five minutes to the bell. I was about to do a

Dionne redial when jarringly, the classroom door banged open and De flew in.

The first thing I noticed was that she hadn't used the extra time to perfect her look. Unless she was going for disheveled. While her trousers were Versace, they were . . . jeans. That is so *un* for school attire. Ditto her off-the-shoulder stretch midriff, minus belly loop. And while Candie's *are* this season's footwear comeback, I would have gone for the Betsey Johnson line, not the Anna Sui. Plus? I had a sneaking suspicion her wraparounds were last semester's Ray•Bans, not this year's Obliques. Okay, so there might be an excuse for momentary ensemble-diversion, but there was none for De's hair. Her extensions were all askew, protruding at grievously quirky angles.

The total picture? Mass distress in De-land.

Without eyeballing any of us, De marched to her seat, dropped her backpack on the floor, flopped down, and cradled her head on the desk.

Profoundly alarmed, I rushed right over.

"De! Are you all right? Should we call your internist? Your guru? Your masseuse?"

But my main big emitted no reply.

Even Murray could tell that whatever was wrong with De was no joking matter. He galloped over to her seat, knocking over Jesse's Humvee catalog in the process, yelling, "Baby, what's the matter?"

Sean tripped over himself to get to De, too.

Amber, unable to risk being left out, made it a crowd.

Unlike other authority figures who might have

resented De's sudden pilfering of the spotlight, Miss Geist hurried over, a ball of concern. "Dionne? Are you ill?"

That's when De looked up. At close range, even with her dark wraparounds, it was immediately apparent De had been wallowing in a total angst fest.

De sniffled and answered Miss Geist. "I'm having a bad mother day."

"Is your mother sick?" Geist wondered, concerned.

Angrily, De lashed out. "I'm the one who's sick—sick of her!"

That was brutally un-De. Normally she and her parental unit were the designer-quality of mother-daughter relationships. They bond by cellular, pager, and E-mail every day. In all my years of t.b.-ship with De, I couldn't remember her having a bad mother day. Her situation had to be beyond 911.

Just then the bell rang, announcing the end of third period. PE would have been next, but, hello, not even. Dionne was clearly in crisis. And what are friends, boyfriends, teachers, and even rivals for, if not support?

Led by Miss Geist, we repaired to the teachers' lunchroom, a desolate space riddled with unadorned tables and metal folding chairs, the final resting place for several coffee pots. We settled in on a threadbare couch and urged De to unburden.

Pacing the room in her strapless, backless Candie's, De described her morning, sacrificed to what Murray adroitly tagged "the home version of the family strife game."

Brandishing a thick, oversize creamy beige envelope embellished with gold calligraphy, De was all,

"See this? This came yesterday, and as any duh-head can see, it is addressed to *me!*"

In my experience? Envelopes like that usually contain furious invitations. It was just like the type that Daddy, a totally prominent attorney, receives weekly for various black-tie, disease-oriented charity balls. As De extracted a stellar gold-bordered multi-layered card out of the envelope, I could see I was right. It *was* an invitation.

"It's from my father's third ex-wife, Chandra," De explained. "She's throwing a week-long open-house family reunion bash to celebrate her stepdaughter's engagement. She invited all branches of the family—including me—to drop in any time during that week."

"De, that is so righteous," I said, admiring Chandra's inclusion instinct. I knew that De hadn't seen this particular ex of her dad's in several years.

Murray chimed, "So what's buggin' you out, baby? That she didn't send a separate invite for your man?"

De ignored Murray's lame attempt at a lighter moment. She fumed, "What's buggin' me out is that *she*—Attila-the-mother—said no. She's banning me from going! What gives her the right to decide whether I can accept an invitation or not?"

"Because she's your mother?" I guessed.

De flashed irate eyes at me. Oops, my bad. My fully supportive gear must have been locked in neutral. I amended. "I mean, did your mother give you, like, back-up data or a reason to support her opposition?"

De harrumphed. "A reason? As if! It was brutally faux! She was all, 'I don't want you fraternizing with that side of the family.' "

"And then," Amber jumped in, "when you said 'Why?' did she say, 'Because I said so'? I mean, that is such a primary parental fallback position. Like when they actually *have* no reason. Once? When I wanted to seize a Dolce & Gabbana black lizard purse, would you believe my mother actually said I couldn't have it, just because she said so? It totally took an overseas call to Daddy, who was all, 'Of course you can, Princess.' "

"Amber!" Like stop her before she soliloquizes. "This isn't about you," I reminded her. "I know this is a major shock, but not everything is."

"Excuse me, Oprah, I know that. I was just being empathetic."

Normally, I would have retorted, "No, Amber, you're just being *pa*thetic," but I let it go. This really was about De, who was still pacing and sliding dangerously in and out of her shoes.

And erupting. "This is beyond obtuse! I don't know what her problem is. This side of the family was like, three divorces and a separation ago. And postscript: Everyone's furiously amicable. Or was."

Miss Geist, who'd been silent so far, offered, "Maybe your mother is just afraid of losing you, Dionne. Even in the best relationships, people sometimes get insecure if they think the other person is changing or growing away from them."

Miss Geist had nailed a rampantly important point. Like why was De's mother so unyielding this time? And what was beneath De's über-bummed-out reaction? And stop tape: What was that faraway misty look in Geist's eyes when she was all that thing about "the other person is changing or growing away from them"?

De dismissed Geist's theory. "Afraid of losing me? As if! This is not a custody thing, it's a visit. I'm fully committed to my mother. Even if, every time she whimsically plays musical husbands, I have to rearrange my life."

Amber crossed her legs and made an exaggerated motion of checking her diamond-and-sapphire-encrusted Gucci timepiece. "Look, Dionne, I don't know why you're angst-festing over this. The solution is as obvious as that errant hair extension protruding toward Saturn. You got an invitation. You want to go. As Cher so brutally pointed out, it's about you. Ergo, just go. When your mother finds out, she'll forgive you. Daddy always forgives me."

I rolled my eyes. "Ergo, just go? Get a grip—and another scriptwriter—Amber. Open defiance is so three decades ago."

"Excuse me, like you've got a better solution?" she challenged.

Everyone eyed me hopefully.

Tragically, I didn't. Not just yet, anyway. But, hello, like even Bart Simpson knows that when it comes to parents, skillful negotiation rules over random tantrums.

"Where is the gala reunion, anyway, De?" I asked.

She totally moaned. "That's the best part. It's at Chandra's beach house—in Hawaii, on Maui. Look, they even sent a picture."

De pulled a colorful snapshot out of the envelope and passed it around. The photo portrayed a furious ocean-view beach house. Its floor-to-ceiling windows overlooked a stellar wraparound bleached-wood deck that came accessorized with chaise longues, mottled-glass-top tables and jaunty sun-blocking umbrellas. A graceful staircase led onto a pristine white sand beach.

"I'm nauseous for you," I responded, admiring the magnificent mansion on the beach that De was being pressured to pass on.

Murray stroked his chin. "Chandra has a beach house in Maui? Wasn't it Gillian with the Hawaii connection?"

De vented. "How long have we been going out, Murray?"

I guessed that was a rhetorical question, since De didn't give her boo a chance to calculate but blasted, "How can you not know this? Gillian was my father's second ex-wife, the one whose brother-in-law got you the discount on those massive woofers for your stereo."

Recognition filled Murray's eyes. "Oh, yeah, I remember now. And she's the one with the stepson who tried out for the Lakers' farm team."

"Hello! *No!* That's Joanna, my father's fiancée before he married Gillian, but broke up with because of the whole pre-nup contretemps," De seethed.

"I'm sorry, Miss Dionne, but yours is the most convoluted family on the map," Murray concluded.

Amber raised her hand in protest. "Excuse me, I don't think so. Dionne's isn't even the most convoluted family in this room. I can say with authority that moi has the only simultaneously, concurrently married parents of our group."

As much as it pained me to agree with Ambulame, her truth was out there. Most of our families *were* complex and multilayered. But like, it's the nineties. And it's Beverly Hills, the attention deficit disorder capital of the world.

But that tangential bit was extraneous to De, who was nearing full hysteria, as she bellowed, "I've *got* to find a way to go!"

My t.b. was desperately in need. And to me? That spells one thing: project!

Chapter 2

I pondered De's dilemma the rest of the day. It was grievously thorny. I mean, most instances of parent-teenager discord revolve around the three C's: curfews, credit cards, and cars. It's the classic conflict between the need on our part for upgrades on all of the above and the need on their part for like, limits. With Daddy and me, there's always room for negotiation, especially if you present compelling evidence to support your case. Or you're really, really good at manipulation.

But in De's case, something else was tugging at me. Maybe Miss Geist was right about De's mom's fear of abandonment. But why was De so wiggin'? What was so intense about this invitation that she couldn't bear a judgment, albeit random, against her? I suspected that I didn't have the total picture. And until I did, coming up with a positive, solution-oriented plan was beyond even me, acclaimed untier of thorny knots.

So every period for the rest of the school day, I beeped De. Eventually, I pieced together the deeper truth of De's absolute need to attend the family reunion.

Over lunch De dropped, "It's in smog-free Hawaii!"

Translation: Several new designer boutiques have opened since De's last island jaunt.

In fifth period De divulged, "I'd need an entire new wardrobe."

Translation: Can you say "shopping ops"?

In sixth period she revealed, "Chandra is an executive at Chanel."

Translation: A renewed relationship spells deep discounts.

In seventh period she confided, "I've got an entire posse of stepsibs I haven't seen in ages. Some are even biologically related."

Translation A: Like me, De lives with one parent and she wants to feel part of a larger DNA-related group. Translation B: De wants to show them up.

By eighth period she totally exhaled. "My father is going to be there, Cher. There was an extra note in the envelope from him. And even though the visitation thing is in full effect, since he lives in Hawaii I really don't see him much."

Like, finally. Now I understand why De's mother is being so hard core. And why De is being such the rebel, determined to go.

* * *

The family thing, especially when it spirals around steprelations, can be massively complicated and uncomfortable. The deeper truth of that in my own life was sprawled all over the apricot sectional in the great room, watching TV when I got home that afternoon.

Josh, the stepbrother from the rainy planet—Seattle, that is—took that Spanish expression *mi casa es su casa* way too literally. And also the addendum about raiding the fridge: he was totally scarfing frozen yogurt straight from the container.

As I tossed my leather cocoa Tignanello slingback, and then myself, on the couch next to him, I demanded, "Remind me again why you're not in school in Seattle? Now that Courtney's gone Hollywood, doesn't the grunge scene need to marshal all its remaining forces?"

Josh barely took his eyes off the TV screen. Scrapping the last of drops of the frappaccino no-fat yogurt, he retorted, "And isn't there a mall not far away writhing in Cher deprivation at this very moment?"

Josh, no biological relation, thank you, is the son of Daddy's fourth wife, Gail. Their legal union, I always remind Daddy, was fully brief. Forty-three days of fractious brevity to be exact.

"So what?" Daddy always reminds me right back. "You divorce wives, not children."

And now that his nonchild Josh was a pre-law student at UCLA, Daddy embraces the concept that Josh spends more time in our spacious Beverly Hills villa than in his cramped and cruddy dorm room. Okay, so the advantages to a normal person are obvious, but Josh and normal are mutually exclusive.

The step-pain, a remnant of the Deny Me decade, proudly wears his struggling student patch on his flannel sleeve. Wasn't this loitering in Beverly Hills akin to mingling with the oppressors? Or something.

"What's got you so riveted?" I asked, eyeballing the big-screen TV. It seemed to be some nature-themed animal documentary. "Or is this a video sent by your newest dating service? Have you run out of human date options already?"

Josh rolled his eyes. "Since any show not hosted by animated characters or supermodels is beyond your grasp, Cher, I wouldn't expect you to recognize this. For your information, it's PBS's *Endangered America.*"

"Oooh, wild! Or is it, groovy? What *is* the lexicon among the deeply hip these days, Josh?"

Josh ignored me, which meant Cher 1, Josh 0 in today's verbal sparring bout. Bored with my easy win, I started to get up, when for the teensiest second, I allowed the TV narrator to pierce my consciousness.

He was saying, "The Hawaiian monk seal is one of the world's last two surviving tropical seals. This living treasure was nearly slaughtered into extinction for its skin and oil but is slowly making a comeback under protected status. The monk seal resides almost exclusively in the uninhabited northwestern Hawaiian islands, though some have come ashore in Maui."

Slowly, I sank back onto the couch. The words "Hawaiian" and "extinct" in the same sentence had a distant joyful ring: like, "Calvin" and "sale," or "credit card" and "unlimited." Separately, they were merely proper, but together? Megadope. And right now they were molting together: the beginnings of a lightbulb, albeit still on the dimmer switch. I needed more wattage.

"Um, you know, Josh, I so have to hand it to you. Your taste in docudrama is beyond impeccable. What other extinct variety of animal did the TV dude say resides in, like, Hawaii?"

Josh shot me a suspicious look. "It's not a docudrama. It's a documentary on rare, endangered species. And why do you care? To you, an endangered species is a credit card nearing its expiration date."

"Hello, give me a little credit beyond plastics, Josh. Did I not so extend my grasp about recyclable wearables—aka, avant garbage—during the Environmental Expo? And about the real world when I totally rocked that magazine internship?"

Josh exhaled. "You know, I'd love to stay and discuss the ever-widening horizons of Cher Horowitz, but I've gotta go. A philosophy paper calls. If you have a burning desire to know more"—Josh aimed the remote at the TV—"I believe a Learn More About It phone number is about to magically appear on screen."

I yanked the remote from him so he couldn't click off the TV. That would be just like Josh. Only this time he offered no resistance but just sauntered off toward the kitchen. He was right, though. A phone number had appeared on the screen, and I scrambled in my slingback to grab a pen. The number was for a group called the Sierra Club. For some reason, the window of Banana Republic flashed through my mind.

I decided to call from my bedroom. Josh wasn't on the need-to-know list about my sudden interest in the Sierra Club. As I crossed the terra-cotta tiles in the foyer toward the staircase, I stopped to say hi to Mom. The portrait of Mom, that is. She died when I was a baby, just after I learned my first two-syllable word: *AmEx.*

Not unlike my friend Dionne, I, too, have a relationship with my maternal parental unit. Only ours sort of transverses that time-space continuum thing. She's like a nonspeaking, featured performer in my life. I tell Mom all about my furiously fabulous life, and she listens. I was about to tell her about my still-forming idea, when I realized she wasn't looking directly at me: hello, Mom was crooked. As I straightened the portrait, I noticed that she felt a little loose, too.

"'Zup, Mom. I'm thinking about a class trip to Hawaii. How does that grab ya?" I try for retrospeak to be sure Mom understands me.

Now that she could see me clearly, Mom seemed to want to know more, so I continued. "See, De needs to bond with her family in Hawaii. And that's where monk seals are. They're way endangered, which is Miss Geist's cause du jour. So I'm thinking field trip. Do you copy?"

I wasn't sure if "do you copy?" was from Mom's era or some police show, but I was pretty sure she thumbs-upped my jammin' idea. I bolted up the steps to call the Sierra Club.

Okay, so after like going through a voice-mail-o-rama of interminable options, during which I think I may have made a massive donation, I finally connected with a human. She vigorously assured me that not only do the monk seals live in Hawaii, but so do other endangered species, like green sea turtles and humpback whales.

"By any chance," I asked tentatively, "does your organization sponsor eco-field trips to, like, financially well-off potential future members of your club?"

Ms. Sierra Club was all perky. "It just so happens we do." There was bodacious information she could send me all about the trips, too, but I told her the Hawaii material was all we needed. I gave her Daddy's Fed Ex account number and the address of Bronson Alcott High School and requested top priority service.

Then I called De. "If this works, girlfriend, you are on your way to Maui."

De was overcome with gratitude. All she could manage was "Wowee!"

The huge package was delivered to me in Miss Geist's class the next day. I asked permission to open it at her desk, assuring our teacher that its contents were related to our endangered species unit.

"But the due date for your presentation isn't for another three weeks, Cher," Miss Geist responded, perplexed at my enthusiasm.

I ripped open the box and turned it upside down. A plethora of videos, books, and pamphlets spilled out. As promised, they were all Hawaii-centric, with videos entitled, "The Plight of the Humpback Whales" and "Sea Turtles and Monk Seals: Hawaii's Endangered Treasures." The book was called *Adventuring in Hawaii: A Sierra Club Travel Guide.*

Geist was all, "I'm impressed at the effort you're

putting into this, Cher, but wasn't your assignment the white rhinoceros?"

"But that's just it, Miss Geist," I said passionately. "It's not about just my small part of the assignment. The whole unit is frantically more important than that. Your passion for this cause has totally inspired me. So last night I undertook extensive research on our class's behalf. Here is what I propose."

I sucked in my breath and looked to De for support. She gave me a solid thumbs up. So did Murray and Sean, Jesse, Ringo, Janet, Summer, Annabelle, and pretty much the rest of our class, all of whom had been clued in earlier in the morning. Only Amber had been left out of the loop: Just to see her reaction, always priceless.

I went into my spiel, which I'd spent the better part of the morning rehearsing. "I, Cher Horowitz, speaking on behalf of your entire third-period social studies class, propose a Sierra Club–sponsored field trip to actually experience such endangered species as the humpback whale, green sea turtle, and monk seal. How else can we can be completely assured of feeling their pain? Such an endeavor would be furiously hands-on and wholly educational."

Miss Geist was often naively passionate about her causes. Sartorially, she totally overlooked form for function. And sometimes she was just plain run-in-her-stockings distracted. But she wasn't a duh-head. Which is why the first words out of her mouth were "I don't suppose the location of this field trip would happen to be . . . oh, say, Hawaii?"

I shrugged. "It just so happens that these heinously endangered marine mammals are, like, unique to the islands of our fiftieth state."

Geist regarded me tentatively. I knew a part of her was proud of me for my capacity to mix and match separates—De's dilemma and the class's better understanding of the whale thing—and come up with a golden solution. But being the authority figure in the room, she couldn't acquiesce instantly.

So I tossed in more. "Our class is profoundly field-trip-impaired. The juniors went to Gstaad; did the seniors not go to Monaco? Even the freshmen went to the gala opening of Bloomingdale's for their field trip. Our trip—proposed trip—is by far the most frantically educational."

Unsurprisingly, Amber's left hand flew up. Like, what had taken her so long? Her other hand was paging through her organizer. When Geist recognized her, Amber was all "Exactly when, I demand to know, do you propose taking this little field trip? And since Cher purports to be speaking on behalf of the entire class, why was I not consulted? I have a brutally congested schedule, which cannot be capriciously altered just because Cher suddenly comes up with a self-serving little scheme."

Naturally, Amber caught onto the Hawaii connection, too. And she so didn't appreciate being out of the loop.

Ignoring her, I continued to offer Miss Geist more reasons to just say yes.

"If you approve this field trip, we'll need at least one other adult chaperon. Maybe Mr. Hall could be sprung for duty."

Something told me Miss Geist and her husband,

our English literature and debate teacher, Mr. Hall, could use a little island paradise in their immediate futures.

Geist sighed and perched on her desk, thumbing through the Sierra Club material. "While I agree in principle with your proposal, Cher, I'll have to take this up with administration. I'll let you know as soon as I know."

After class, De, Amber and I rushed up to tête-a-tête with our teacher, discussing which week would be most convenient for all of us to go. The time frame we agreed on just so happened to coincide with the week of De's Hawaiian family reunion.

Everything hinged on getting the school's thumbs-up.

Chapter 3

It took a few juliette-trashing days before we heard back from Miss Geist. But the morning we entered the classroom to find her and Mr. Hall together, we knew the news had to be massively righteous.

As soon as we took our seats, Miss Geist advised us, "Mr. Hall and I have an exciting announcement. The administration has approved the Sierra Club–sponsored field trip to Hawaii, but—"

Her "but" was momentarily obscured by the cheering, whooping, and cacophonous modem-connecting noises of our classmates who needed to make prompt E-mail appointments with their personal shoppers in preparation for the trip. I, of course, had to receive my snaps, which came in the form of applause, hugs, and the so-far-unreleased Alanis EP that Jesse tossed my way: the ultimate gracias from our most pompous and well-connected-to-the-music-biz classmate. Not to mention the one who won't give up on the brutally faux idea that I would ever consider going out with him. Though I did keep the Alanis.

With Mr. Hall's help, Geist eventually reclaimed our attention.

She explained. "Because we've narrowed our focus to marine life in Hawaii, we now have the time and resources to do a more in-depth study. Therefore, Mr. Hall and I have decided to alter your assignment. Instead of each of you reporting on a different endangered animal, you will all work together, preparing a video documentary on the threats to Hawaii's marine life population. It will be an exercise in cooperation, as well as a wonderful learning experience."

De, who was beyond psyched at the turn of events, leaped out of her seat, enthusing, "A documentary! Just like *Unzipped!*"

Miss Geist was unfamiliar with that reality-based Isaac Mizrahi fashion film. Still, she and Mr. Hall appreciated De's enthusiasm.

Sean waved his arm frantically. "Miss Geist! Miss Geist! Does this mean I don't have to do those hoop dreams birds?"

"You may report on whooping cranes for extra credit, Sean, but you will be getting a new assignment on our marine life documentary," Geist detailed. "In fact, Mr. Hall, who has graciously agreed to chaperon with me"—she smiled coyly at her main—"will now explain more about that."

"Thank you, my dear," Mr. Hall acknowledged his

beloved. Then our other favorite teacher cleared his throat and explained that making a documentary was similar to making a movie.

"There are several parts to fill. We'll need a director, cinematographer, narrator, several writers and researchers—"

But he didn't get through his list of parts, because twenty hands immediately shot into the air. Few waited to be recognized but yelled out,

"I'm calling my agent!"

"I'm calling my publicist!"

"I'm calling my entertainment lawyer!"

And twenty cell phones were whipped out as my peers began speed dialing their various representatives.

Amber, of course, was all, "Excuse me, since I have valuable on-air experience, I believe that qualifies me to be the on-air talent."

De challenged her. "As if! If you're talking about that *Hard Copy*-esque exposé we did nailing the thief in Nordstrom's, hello, that was *me* on camera. You were behind the scenes."

As Amber rushed to contradict De and bring me in on the fracas, Mr. Hall called for decorum.

"People! People! While Miss Geist and I are thrilled with the level of eagerness you're showing, she and I, as executive producers, will be handing out the parts. And there will be no discussion. Our decisions are final."

Amid the grumbling, grousing, and that's-not-fairing, Mr. Hall and Miss Geist took command. In fact, the rest of the period was devoted to giving out assignments and permission slips. Naturally, we needed parental okays. A minor detail. Like anyone's parents would object. Even De's mother had to stamp Approved on the trip or risk compromising De's education.

At the end of class, a horde of my peers, dissatisfied with their assignments, rushed Mr. Hall. Even though he had said all parts were final sale, no returns or exchanges, it was way a mosh pit of student negotiators angling for more glamorous roles. I heard snippets of complaints: "A grip? I can't be a grip! I have tennis elbow!" And "What is best boy? Don't you mean best-dressed boy?"

We were a majorly fractious class. Geist and Hall really expected us to work together?

Still, I was so majorly psyched, my cheekbones ached from being locked in the smile position. I barely noticed that I'd gotten the less than on-camera-y part of writer. De had snared the even lower profile researcher. She was thinking of lobbying for makeup artist when I reminded her that the stars of the documentary were, in fact, sea creatures, better filmed au naturel.

Sean was named property master. He thought that meant real estate agent to the stars. "Not even," De enlightened him. "You're responsible for the props, Sean—as in accessories, not snaps."

In fact, of our immediate posse, it was Murray, Jesse, and, grievously, Amber, who'd actually snared the ripest parts. Murray was chief cinematographer and Jesse had landed director's stripes. Already he was on one phone to Quentin Tarantino for advice, and on another making a deal for the soundtrack. I overheard him saying, "Think *Independence Day* with a whale . . . yeah, like *Free Willy.*"

Heinously, Amber ended up getting exactly what she wanted: narrator.

Even that couldn't put a damper on all I had accomplished. Thanks to my classic solution, De could now legally bypass her mother's objections and freely debut at her family reunion. And, bonus! Since our school graciously comps chaperons, Mr. Hall and Miss Geist snared a stress-free, all expenses-paid, island paradise vacation.

And we were going to—hello—Hawaii, a smog-free theme park of upscale boutiques and high-maintenance endangered animals. Not to mention sun, sand, and beach Baldwins.

I was still giving myself major snaps when Miss Geist approached me and De. I thought she was going to thank us for not kvetching about our low-glam assignments, but not even.

Gently, she warned, "Look, Dionne. I know the real reason you want to go is to see your family, but I can't guarantee that will happen. There is some free time built into the trip, but for the most part, we'll be on a tight Sierra Club schedule. And besides, I can't really condone your disobeying your mother. I'd feel better if you got her okay."

Which De did. Basically.

She buzzed her mom from her next class and beeped me afterward.

"I went for classic casual," De described. "I didn't say one word about Chandra and the beach house thing. I emphasized the trip's eco-purpose and fully mentioned that we'd be chaperoned and snugly scheduled at all times."

"And she caved?" I asked, incredulous that it had been that easy.

"Like Amber at a discount Gucci sale," De said, buzzed about her coup. "I ran to the guidance office and faxed her the permission slip and she signed it and faxed it back. Now, Cher, all that's left is the shopping!"

"Girlfriend! We start tomorrow," I agreed.

I waited until I got home to do the permission thing with Daddy. Not that he wouldn't green-light my going. Daddy and I just did better with interfaces.

The first thing I noticed as I swung into our cobblestone driveway later that afternoon was the absence of Josh's Jeep Laredo. It put me in a better mood than I already was, which I didn't think possible.

But hello, I also didn't think it was possible for Daddy to have even a micro objection to the trip. That's where I had to do a think redial.

"Aloha, my all-time favorite daddy," I greeted him jauntily as I danced into his study. Being in the way upper echelons of his profession gives Daddy the chance to operate Mel Horowitz & Associates from home as well as from his office downtown.

He was standing at his mahogany desk, barking orders over the phone to one of his associates, while several other lines blinked for his attention. I tiptoed around his desk and gave him a peck on the cheek as he thundered into the speaker, "I said I needed a full deposition from the ex-wife, not some cockamamie statement. And I said I needed it yesterday! Not tomorrow!"

Daddy slammed down the phone and sighed.

"Sorry, sweetheart. How was school? And by the way"—he snapped shut his appointment book and peered at me intently—"what do you want?"

"Daddy," I admonished, "what makes you think I want anything?"

"Well, don't you?" he asked in that faux-gruff way Daddy has. "Whenever you greet me as your favorite all-time daddy, it usually means I have to reach for my checkbook. So I'm wrong this time?"

Daddy threw me a fully indulgent, yet skeptical, look.

I grinned. "Well, okay. You're not exactly wrong. I do need something, but you're going to be majorly psyched, because it's for educational purposes."

Daddy sank into his studded leather swivel chair, leaned back, and crossed his arms behind his head. "I can't wait, Cher. I don't think I've been 'majorly psyched' in let's see . . ." He consulted his Tag Heuer. "Probably not since you left for school this morning and left me with a cork coaster you tried to pass off as a rice cake. So, counselor, present your case. Psych me out."

When I finished detailing the purpose and timing of our class field trip, I expected Daddy to be all, "Whale watching with the Sierra Club! I remember when I was your age . . ."

Not even. Instead of regaling me with quasi-related tales of his youth, Daddy furrowed his brow. Translation: anxiety rules. Oh, doy, I'd forgotten how his protective vibe kicks in whenever I mention leaving the zip code.

"I don't know, Cher. Your track record for out-of-state trips isn't exactly without incident. You've got some priors."

Okay, so that time in New York my luggage got stolen. And Daddy wouldn't let me go to Paris without bunking at relatives', and even then my friend's passport got stolen.

"But this trip is different," I reminded him. "It's fully chaperoned and sanctioned by our school. And aren't you forgetting everything worked out when I went to that school-sponsored outdoor spa encounter?"

"Wait a minute, Cher," Daddy interrupted me. He hunched forward in his chair and consulted his organizer. "What week did you say the trip was?"

When I pointed out our time frame, all of a sudden Daddy seemed to relax. "Look, Cher, I admit I am a little overprotective. I can't help being nervous when you're away. But it's a parent's inalienable right to be nervous. You're my little girl. And besides, I'm in the middle of the Kassan case, which means I could be called away to New York at any moment. But now that I see what week it is, you have my permission to go. Knowing your brother will be there the same week gives me peace of mind."

"My bro— *What?*" I couldn't believe what I was hearing.

Daddy was all, "Josh has no classes that week. Some of his fraternity brothers booked a trip to Hawaii, and he decided to join them. What a neat coincidence, don't you think? Cher, why are you looking at me like that?"

My previously happy face had decomposed into a mask of ick. This unexpected wrinkle, minuscule though it was, left me momentarily off balance. And severely unthrilled.

Daddy was all, "So where do I sign? You still want to go, don't you?"

Quickly, I regained my composure. "Duh, of course I do, Daddy." I fished out the permission slip from my Cynthia Rowley mini-tote, and Daddy signed on the dotted line. I gave him a significant hug. Then I mentioned to him about Mom's portrait seeming a little loose to me. He said he'd check on it.

I took my emotional pulse as I started up the stairs to call De. Okay, I was buggin' about the Josh thing, but keeping my eyes on the prize is one of my strong suits. And at the end of the day? Daddy had signed off on it. And hello, I reminded myself, Hawaii is a whole bunch of islands. What are the chances I'll be side-swiped by the stepmonster?

"Cher, I woke up this morning and suddenly realized I could not live one more second without a pair of Richard Tyler relaxed but rumpled drawstring pants!" De was exclaiming. She, Amber, and I were power shopping the Galleria mall the next day after school in preparation for our Hawaiian holiday. Field trip, that is.

Earlier we'd spent our lunch break alongside our co-stars, including Summer, Janet, Annabelle, Ringo, Murray, Sean, and Jesse at our regular VIP table in our outdoor dining area, aka the Quad. We huddled over books, brochures, and CD-ROMs detailing Hawaii's wildly divergent terrain and atmospheric pressures. We'd need to pack cosmetic supplies for all variables.

" 'Hawaii is home to both the world's most active volcano and most dormant volcano'," De had read out of the guide book.

"Sounds like a serious lava-fest," I'd noted as I picked through a plate of spring rolls catered by ObaChine, the hot new Pacific Rim cuisine bistro.

"I'm packing my lava lamp!" Sean declared over his Arch Deluxe. We didn't bother to respond but tried to determine what type of ensemble would go best when posed next to a volcano, either active or dormant.

De, noshing on a croissandwich, continued. " 'There you find rain forests, including the wettest spot on earth, side by side with parched deserts.' "

"That totally plays havoc with the moisturizer situation," Summer fretted.

"We'll need a bodacious variety of lip glosses to combat the environment," Janet added, "plus a mix of essential proteins, ceramids, and lipids for skin nourishment."

"Forget about that," Murray, sipping an Arizona Iced Tea, joked. "Get to the part about those Hawaiian Tropics girls. Where you do find them?"

De shot him a dagger and continued, " 'Trade winds caress the body.' "

Horrified, all the Bettys screamed in unison, "Our hair!"

We added extra conditioners and mousses to our mental list of supplies, already longer than Miss Geist's endangered species list.

Luckily, growing up as Beverly Hills Bettys, we all have four-octave ranges in shopping. Today the Galleria. Tomorrow the Beverly Center. Then we'd do Via Rodeo for designer, Melrose for funky, and maybe stretch all the way to Santa Monica for accessories with a beachy POV.

De was determined that she and Murray would meet all branches of her family tree ably attired. On Murray's behalf, we were doing the new Jon Valdi Boutique, an emporium of haute hipster.

At the mall we'd chosen Victoria's Secret as our first stop for their raging swimwear line. Great shopping-minded Bettys think alike, since in the dressing room we ran into Janet, Summer, and Annabelle. We took turns modeling our picks. It was, like, Bronson Alcott High School, the Swimsuit Edition.

Later, we hit Nordstrom's for cosmetics, sweeping through the M.A.C., Bobbi Brown, François Nars, and Laura Mercier counters, picking up custom foundations, cutting-edge cantaloupe-colored blush, and that two-thousand-calorie mascara.

By the time we'd swung through Bath & Bodyworks, Bisou Bisou, BeBe, and XOXO, we were way shopping-bag laden. Fulfilled but also thirsty, I suggested a frappaccino upload.

"Let's hit the Kona Konnection," De agreed as Amber whipped out her cell phone to reserve a table and place our order. Only when we got there, it turned out we needed larger accommodations: our party of three quickly expanded to six as we bumped into Murray, Sean, and Jesse.

"Hey, boo." De, her spirits flying, greeted Murray with a mouth-to-cheek connection.

Murray greeted her with a correction. "No more boo for me, baby. From now on you can call me the Big Kahuna. I don't know about you flighty femmes, but I'm taking my new career seriously. Look here." Murray indicated his shopping bag from the Camera Barn. "I stocked up on cinematography supplies. I bought a high-tech video camera—an endangered species cam, if you will—film for all vicissitudes of lighting, and canisters for safe storage. See, I remember all that stuff from Cher's last boyfriend, that camera whiz, Matt. I'm all set."

As De laughed and smooched her big kahuna again, I felt a twinge of nostalgia for Matt, with whom I'd shared a brief but furiously emotional few weeks. All too soon, he'd returned to his home in Nebraska. My hottie just before him, Aldo, was even farther away, back in his stomping grounds, Italy. I guessed east wasn't my direction when it came to relationships. Fortunately, Hawaii was west. And who knew what species of sand 'n' surf studmuffin awaited me there?

As if he could read my mind—the one dreaming of potential new Baldwins to strive for—Jesse broke in. "Want to see what I got, Cher?"

The answer, "Not really," sprang to my lips, but before I could get it out, Jesse dumped the contents of several shopping bags on our table. Unlike Murray, Jesse had bought zilch for his important directorial debut. Instead, he'd filled up on surfing accoutrements, including Amber-esque sun glasses—the ones with mirrors on the inside—so handy for self-admiration. Then Jesse held up a pair of severely low-cut Speedos and went smarmy. "Bet you can't wait to see me in these, Cher."

"Bet I can," I countered.

Amber, piqued that she wasn't part of the conversation, broke in. "Excuse me, you're not the only one who acquired supplies. We did, too."

"Represent, ladies," Sean encouraged.

We displayed our cosmetics, ensembles, and bathing suits for the boys. Jesse was foaming at the mouth, but Murray was all, "That bikini rocks, woman, but not in any seaworthy Amy Van Dyken–Jacques Cousteau manner, you know what I'm sayin'?"

De giggled. "Who said anything about going in the water? These are for posing *by* the water."

Then she went all flirty. "Hey, Big Kahuna, think you'll have any film left in your camera to capture me live on tape? I am way endangered!"

Murray broke into a major grin, and he and De began canoodling.

I turned to Sean, who seemed shopping-bag-impaired.

"Don't tell me you're saving your plastic for Hawaii?" I teased.

"Au contraire, Cher. I bought the most important tool I'll need for conversing with the Hawaiian Tropics ladies." Sean pulled a Hawaiian guidebook out of his backpack. "It's got a section that translates Hawaiian to English."

Amber rolled her eyes. "This just in, Sean. We

annexed Hawaii several decades ago. *Hablan inglés* there."

Sean shook his head. "Not for everything, Amber. I did research. There is an official Hawaiian language. And if you really want to communicate with the natives, you gotta speak it. Check this. Define: *aliloa.*"

Amber yawned. "As my Dandie Dinmont puppy could tell you, and correct your pronunciation at the same time, it means 'hello,' Sean. And 'good-bye.' Take the book back, you got rooked."

"See, Amber, you're wrong already! *Aloha* means 'hello,' 'good-bye,' 'peace,' and a bunch of stuff. *Aliloa* refers to an ancient highway, usually around the coastal circumference of an island. So there!"

"That was massively need to know, Sean," Amber deadpanned. "Know what else? I saw a money-changing booth downstairs. Maybe you can get a favorable rate exchanging dollars for Hawaiian currency."

I sipped my decaf frappaccino and took in the whole scene. All my t.b.'s were together, shopping for a common cause: our upcoming trip to Hawaii. De and Murray were lip-locking. Amber and Jesse were mired in self-admiration. Sean was studying up on Hawaiian words to meet girls.

Like, all was right with the world.

Chapter 4

Leaving LA had been furiously bon voyagey, as a lineup of limo-bearing, teary-eyed parents armed with video cameras had come to see us off. It was massively heart-tugging, as we stepped onto the tarmac leading to the private plane Annabelle's father had chartered for us. En route we snacked on sushi from Sushi-rama and personal pizzas from Spago Beverly Hills, then saw an advance screening of the new Tom Cruise movie.

Who would have believed, not quite six hours later, nostalgia for parents and our normal perks had all but completely faded? For the minute we landed on the Hawaiian island of Maui, a bodacious tropical paradise, we were awash in the spirit of Aloha. Before we even boarded the luxury hotel-bound tour bus, we were greeted by a flotilla of welcome wagon natives who adorned us with traditional leis, necklaces of fresh, fragrant flowers. Only Amber quibbled with the one she got. She was all, "Excuse me, like this matches my outfit?"

De and I sniffed the air. It was filled with sweet scents, courtesy of a massive profusion of foliage. It made us only a little homesick for smog. I quipped, "I don't think we're in Kansas anymore, Dionne."

As we were spirited to our hotel, I scanned the scenery. Maui seemed to be such the cutting-edge mix of furious mountainsides, verdant valleys, and coco palm beaches. A manicured oasis of über-luxury resort hotels hugged the shoreline. Best of all was our hotel. It was way Maui 90210. A Josh-free zone for sure.

The Grand Hyatt Wailea, a mega-resort, wasn't one of the usual bases for Sierra Club tours, but since Janet's father was a major stockholder, it was our most obvious accommodation option. Family connections are always classic. And serendipitously? It was way amenity-enhanced and fully met our needs. The hotel boasted Maui's best-equipped spa, which offered massages, facials, mud baths, weight training, steam rooms, milk baths, and aromatherapy sessions. We went all ASAP making reservations.

Outside, the pool system, comprised of slides, waterfalls, grottoes, and rapids, wound around the entire sprawling hotel compound.

Naturally, covered cabanas dotted the entire area.

So did, I noticed, extra-buff, bronzed towel boys.

Our rooms afforded massively luxe ocean views.

Tragically, De and I had to share chambers with Amber. Otherwise, we would have felt right at home.

But not even the specter of a week of Ambu-lament, up close and personal, could dampen De's spirits. As soon as we checked in, De whipped out her cellular to make first contact with her clan.

"I got them!" she exulted a few minutes later, bouncing up and down on the bed.

"You got what? The strappy thongs?" Amber, clueless as usual and claiming the largest bureau for her wardrobe, surmised absentmindedly.

"I reached Chandra! I spoke to my father!" De was massively kvelling. "They're all there, all the cousins, stepsiblings, everyone. They gave me directions to the beach house. It's right off some sightseeing trail called the Road to Hana. They can't wait to see me!"

"Did you give them an ETA for your debut?" I asked.

"Not precisely. But I'm pretty sure that Road to Hana thing is part of our tour. So as soon as we can break away . . . you'll go with me, Cher, won't you?"

I sensed a tension in De's voice that hadn't been there since the day she told us about the invitation. Now that we were so close, was my main big panicking? I didn't get a chance to ask, though, because Amber was all, "Naturellement, we'll be there, Dionne. What are friends for?"

De and I exchanged t.b. glances, and shrugged. We made the W sign.

I'd just pulled out my phone to check in stateside

with Daddy when we heard a knock on the door. De opened it to reveal Murray, Sean, and Jesse.

Or what appeared to be the three most righteous members of the Crew. For Bronson Alcott's finest had wasted no time going "native"—that is, they were fully lei-charged, had shed their Hush Puppies for basic barefoot, and around their Speedos had decked themselves out in grass skirts. We'd have barely recognized them if Murray had not been toting his video camera, Sean his translation book, and Jesse his Discman.

"Aloha, wahines!" Sean sang out the Hawaiian word for women. "Care to join us by the pool for a dip?"

Amber was about to slam the door on them, when Murray stopped her. "Not so fast. This is a command performance. Mr. Hall and Miss Geist request the honor of your presence in Hawaii's great out of doors. We are to meet our official Sierra Club guide, who has prepared an orientation speech for us."

"Already?" I asked. "I mean, we just got here. We haven't even finished unpacking."

"We have," Jesse said, "and you've got a half hour. By the way, as a public service, may I remind you to set your watches back three hours. We are in a new time zone, ladies. See ya' in thirty."

In any time zone, we were more accomplished at speed-dialing than speed-dressing. Still, De, Amber, and I managed some semblance of sartorial savvy for our poolside debut. We covered our still limp-from-the-trip hairdos under floppy wide brims and threw wrap-around tops and sarongs over our fresh bathing suits. I went for a strappy mule sandal; De, a Prada platform, and Amber, her Manolo Blahnik floral stiletto-heeled sandals.

As we pirouetted in front of the mirror one last time before leaving the room, we gave ourselves snaps: we were island stylin' already.

In fact, so was our entire contingent. Our classmates, virtually indistinguishable from the other well-heeled tourists staying at the hotel, were already ringing the pool area when we got there. Everyone, except for our grass-skirted three stooges, totally blended with the ambience. I waved to Baez, Brian, Jasmine, Jackson, and Ringo, as well as our Farsi-speaking classmates. Summer and Jesse were on their cellulars, while Janet and Annabelle were stretched out on chaise longues, availing themselves of poolside pedicures.

Sean was trying out his Hawaiian phrases on various hotel staffers, including the pedicurists. Most smiled indulgently but didn't seem to know what Sean was saying. Several pointed to his grass skirt and laughed.

Murray was massively dedicated, totally filming everything.

As De, Amber, and I settled into cabanas for the most excellent sunning position, and began dousing ourselves with SPF 30 sunblock, we noticed Mr. Hall and Miss Geist arriving, accessorized with a tall, well built, sandy-haired dude.

"People, people!" Mr. Hall, forgetting he wasn't at Bronson Alcott, waved his hands and signaled for our attention. While several small children stopped splashing in the pool—clearly, "people, people," had global recognition perception—we knew for whom this teacher called: he was totally trolling for us.

Grievously, we swung away from the sun and focused our attention teacherward.

Miss Geist motioned to the folliclely enhanced dude they were with, who towered over both of them.

"I'd like to introduce Mr. Talbot, our Sierra Club guide for the week," she said with a smile. "He's going to give us a brief orientation."

Mr. Talbot favored Miss Geist with a toothy grin. "It's all right. You can call me Chad."

Call me mental, or maybe I'd gotten too much sun already, but I know what I saw: Geist blushed vigorously. I took stock. Khakied to the max, Chad was thirtyish and furiously safariesque. I suddenly understood why that vision of Banana Republic had come to me when I first heard of the Sierra Club. It was prescient. Chad could have stepped out of the store window.

"Well," he began as Geist and Hall settled into chairs next to him, "why don't I start by telling you a little about the Sierra Club and what you can expect to see on this tour?"

No one had any objection. Nor much interest. As Chad consulted his notes and began his spiel about the eco-purpose of the club, my peers assumed normal classroom behavior. To the sounds of digits being punched into phones, modems connecting, and pedicures proceeding, Amber raised her hand.

"Yes," Chad acknowledged, surprised and pleased

that he'd gotten a reaction already. "Did you have a question?"

"Excuse me, would you mind moving a little? You're blocking the sun."

Astonished, Chad nonetheless shifted to the right.

I nudged Dionne. "Let's do polite. He's kind of cute."

De was all, "He's kind of old, Cher. But . . . whatever." She and I sat up and went all attention-charged as Murray filmed away.

"The humpback whales are Maui's most famous endangered species," Chad announced. "Once hunted nearly to extinction, this awesome and mysterious mammal, which migrates annually from Alaska to Hawaii, is now able to swim in waters protected under federal law. Yet the humpbacks are still under threat from whalers and polluters."

Chad paused to see what effect, if any, his speech was having. He seemed profoundly grateful to De and me, though a bit piqued that Murray was videotaping him.

"I tell you what, young man," he said to Murray. "Why not save your film for tomorrow? That's when we will actually see breaching whales on our first tour."

Jesse raised his hand. For a split second I thought he might actually have something directorial to ask about tomorrow's eco-journey, but not even. What was I thinking? Jesse's mind was on tonight, not tomorrow. And it had to do with socializing, not documenting. He was all, "Miss Geist? Can we go out tonight? There's a slammin' Hard Rock Café in town."

Several of our group boisterously seconded Jesse's request, which Geist reluctantly granted. Then she, Hall, and Chad caucused amongst themselves, nailing down the details of the next day's itinerary. I settled back in my chaise longue and turned toward the sun. As its gentle rays caressed my face, I overheard De telling Murray about her kin connection, while Jesse and Sean phoned the front desk to order rental Jeeps.

Amber was snoring.

The next morning we were rudely awakened by the jarring sound of the phone ringing.

"What's that noise?" De crabbily demanded as I reached for it.

"It's our wake-up call," I responded groggily, picking the receiver up, then setting it down again.

"Wake-up call? Excuse me, we're on vacation," Amber growled, rolling over.

"Excuse me, we're not." I yawned. "We're on safari. Or whale watch. Or something. Grievously, we must sacrifice beauty sleep to the wake-up deities."

No one moved. Without competition, I beat my t.b.'s to the shower and ordered up a healthy room service breakfast for one and all. I couldn't blame De and Amber for carving out extra pillow time, though. Last night had been, as advertised, classic. We'd piled into our rented open-air Jeeps—which reminded me of Josh's Laredo convertible—and convoyed into Maui's main shopping drag in the town of Lahaina.

It had once been a fishing village, Sean knowledgeably related from his guide book, but had transformed itself into an artsy, boutique-filled disco haven. There were all sorts of historic sights that Mr. Hall and Miss Geist—along with Chad—availed themselves of, but my t.b.'s and I concerned ourselves primarily with retail pursuits. We picked up several Avanti retro silk aloha shirts, Maui Monkey backpacks, and a must-have King Kamehameha lampshade at the whimsically dubbed Traders of the Lost Art.

We walked past a humongo tree, whose branches grew downward and into the ground. Remembering Amber's pathetic "living rain forest" presentation at our Environmental Expo, I pegged it as a banyan tree. "The world's largest," Sean advised, reading. Murray filmed it for local color.

We almost diverged into a whitewashed structure optimistically named Baldwin House. But grievously, it turned out to be a museum, not a studmuffin sanctuary.

Deciding where to eat dinner caused our first close-to-postal contretemps. Summer and Annabelle wanted an authentically Hawaiian restaurant, Amber insisted on waterfront dining, while Jesse lobbied frantically for the Hard Rock Café. We eventually compromised on the excellent Cheeseburger in Paradise, which featured a live band. I would have danced, but it was all I could do to keep Jesse at bay. We totally capped off our first night in Hawaii in the way indigenous Planet Hollywood, Maui.

Perhaps it was our late night, or the ravages of jet lag, but De and Amber weren't the only cranky Bronson Alcottians the next morning. When we regrouped in the lobby, even Miss Geist and Mr. Hall seemed a bit frayed around the edges. In fact, the only person who looked none the worse for wear was Chad. Our tour guide had gone all rugged-chic, from his khaki hiking shorts, which ended just above the knee to reveal well-defined calf cuts, to his thick-soled Timberlands.

His choice of attire was, grievously, a clue to today's mode of whale encounter. Naturally, my peers and I assumed we'd be documenting the woefully endangered mammals from the top deck of a luxury cruise liner.

Not even. Our first whale encounter was to take place in dry dock, from atop an actual mountain, which we were heinously expected to hike up.

"We're headed for Puu Olai," Chad informed us, "the best spot on Maui for offshore whale watching. But it can be a bit of a tough climb, so I suggest that those of you who aren't wearing hiking boots go back to your rooms and change."

"This is bogus," Jesse groused. "There are cruises right out of Lahaina—we saw them last night."

"Well, son, the Sierra Club does it this way," Chad good-naturedly replied. "Miss Geist tells me you're doing a documentary, so I suggest you gather up your equipment, since I can pretty much guarantee a heck of a sighting."

I could pretty much guarantee that Chad was aiming most of his comments at Miss Geist. I hoped Mr. Hall wasn't attuned.

Jesse, Amber, and several others registered their opposition, but Mr. Hall and Miss Geist valiantly prevailed. After changing to requisite designer hiking boots—except for De, who insisted her Candie's slides were the only thing she'd brought that matched her shorts outfit—we piled into our Jeep convertibles and followed our fearless leaders to the foot of Puu Olai. It turned out to be a vertically enhanced cinder cone. Our destination was its peak.

"So, is everybody prepared?" Chad asked as we reluctantly de-Jeeped and stared upward. "Stay together and stay on the trail—it's three-hundred sixty feet high. Your lovely teacher, Miss Geist, and I will be up front. Mr. Hall will bring up the rear. Make sure you don't lose sight of us."

It was an arduous trudge-fest. The sun was hot, but those as-advertised trade winds kept the sweat away. And in spite of our opposition to this mode of whale watching, I can proudly say that almost all members of our troupe took our jobs seriously once we got into it.

I'd stuffed my journal, a pink-feather-tipped pen, and a bottle of Evian in my Prada. A writer's tools. De had her research Ray•Bans on, Murray toted the endangered species cam as Sean searched for props and interfaced with Summer, our set director.

Even Amber seemed to remember why we were here. She insisted on carrying a mini microphone to record her parts. But we hadn't climbed halfway up before she started complaining. "Who is our lighting director? How am I supposed to narrate our docudrama if I don't know how I'm lit?"

Only our erstwhile director wasn't giving his all to the project. Jesse, wearing his Discman headphones, seemed to be trapped somewhere between Mellon Collie and the Infinite Sadness. He was having, he explained, a total Pumpkins epiphany. And vegetables ruled over mammals. Whatever.

Finally, just as it seemed we could traipse no more, we arrived chez top. And like Chad had said? The view was massively luxe. And that was just of the beach below. The ocean beyond, tragically, was whale-challenged. While I appreciated the buff wind surfers in the distance, there wasn't much to, like, document.

I was about to make note of that to De, when suddenly, I heard her scream, followed by the sound of my main big making scraping contact with the side of a mountain.

"Ooww! Help! Murray!" she wailed as she went down, butt first.

Murray rushed over to help De, but when he noticed her footgear, one of which had slid off completely and was rolling down the mountain on its own, his sympathy morphed into antipathy.

"What's wrong with you, woman? This is a mountain climbing expedition, not a disco! No wonder you're such a klutz. Serves you right for wearing those trash-flash, slipperlike appendages!"

"And what makes you such an L. L. Bean–head? What would you know?" De fired back at him as he helped her up. "You think bag and sag is the fashion equivalent of all-weather radials!"

I didn't have to hear any more to predict what was going to happen. It always happened exactly this way: our classmates divided like the Red Sea, taking sides with the altercating couple. The boys cheered Murray on, while the girls rallied around De.

Somewhere, above the fray, we heard Chad.

"There! Over there!" he called out. "Did you get it?"

"Did we get what?" Murray spun around.

"The pod! There's an entire family group of humpback whales out there, spouting and fluking."

Chad was right. I moved closer to get a better view. I could see what looked like a mother whale with what Chad pointed out was a newborn beside her. They were leaping high above the waves in a golden arches pattern. They were furiously symmetrical, carefree, and so cute! The thought of pollution poisoning their play was massively sad.

I whipped out my pencil to take notes. Grievously, I was the only one paying attention. The rest of our human pod was way too embroiled in the De-Murray contretemps, which now had the added ingredient of De making Murray miss the best video shot of the day.

Suddenly, we heard our second scream of the day, this one more furiously bloodcurdling than De's. Everyone whipped around in the direction it was coming from.

"Ow! Oh, oh, ouch! It's hot! Help!" It sounded a lot like . . . Mr. Hall?

We all raced toward the sound. Apparently in an effort to get a better view, he'd wandered off the beaten track toward the other side of the mountain. Only there must have been some lavalike substance there that he stepped into. Because when we saw him, poor Mr. Hall was bouncing around on one foot, clutching the other in pain.

Miss Geist and Chad were the first to reach him.

Alarmed, Geist cried, "Alfonse, what is it? What's the matter?"

"It's my foot. I think it's burned!" he yelled.

Chad took charge. He found a boulder for Mr. Hall to sit on while he inspected the damage. The sole of Mr. Hall's shoe was totally burned through.

"It's okay, Mr. Hall, don't worry," Chad said reassuringly. "I know exactly what this is, and I brought a first aid kit." As Chad extracted salve and bandages from his backpack, he explained, "You must have stepped into a lava tube. I didn't realize there were any here. And this isn't even *pahoehoe,* the smooth flowing kind, but *A'a.* You're not the first tourist to mistake one for the other, cut your shoes, and burn your feet. But it's not serious. I've seen worse."

As he heroically helped a hobbling Mr. Hall back down the mountain, I couldn't help but feel Miss Geist seemed more appreciative toward Chad than empathetic toward her husband. She was actually making excuses for Mr. Hall, explaining that Alfonse was so not the adventurer.

Murray and Sean aided shoe-impaired De down Puu Olai, bickering profusely all the way.

Between Mr. Hall's injury and De's unplanned slippage? Our whale watch ended up totally partial.

Back at the hotel, Chad and Miss Geist sought medical attention for Mr. Hall, while the rest of us repaired to the pool area, seeking respite from our first massively draining eco-tour. By that time, De and Murray, too tired to fight anymore, had made up and were canoodling under a cabana.

Later Miss Geist and Chad came out to talk to us. Because of Mr. Hall's injury, he'd have to spent the next few days off his feet and in bed. But Miss Geist didn't want him to miss the other eco-significant parts of the trip, so Chad had graciously agreed to rearrange our itinerary. Instead of scoping green sea turtles and monk seals tomorrow, we'd shift that to the end of the week.

Instead, tomorrow we would do one of the scheduled sightseeing trips: the Road to Hana.

Chapter 5

I assumed De was too busy forgiving Murray for his sympathy-impaired reaction to her mountain mishap to hear Miss Geist's change in plans bulletin. Not even. De untangled herself from Murray and came flying over to me.

"Did you hear that, Cher? The Road to Hana! That means we can segue to the beach house tomorrow!"

Hurriedly, De summoned a poolside waiter to bring her a portable phone. She dialed the spa. "I need emergency appointments," she detailed. "Yes, for a facial, I need to have my hair done, my nails buffed . . ."

In fact, we had to do a room service dinner, as De spent most of that night anxiously modeling various ensembles in preparation for her now imminent *mishpucha* encounter—one of De's Yiddish expressions, meaning "the whole extended family" will be there.

I made a stab at levity as I picked up a pile of discarded outfits and hung them back in the closet. "Girlfriend, chill. You're massively above-the-title just being you. You don't need to dress to impress."

Murray dittoed. "Cher's right, woman. All you need to do is show up. You'll be the belle of the beach, the diva of the dive shop."

But De's frenzy knew no bounds. "Have the Jeep washed," she instructed Murray, "and go to your room and pack the Jon Valdi outfit Cher and I bought you. But also bring the matching Zegna shirt and tie. I'll decide later which one you'll wear when we meet them."

As Murray rolled his eyes and started to leave, De was all, "The map! Did you get a good map of the island? Chandra said it's a little tricky finding the beach house."

Murray put his hands up in protest. "I don't need a map. Chandra told you how to get there, right? You wrote down the directions. That's all I need."

De was buggin'. She warned, "If you get us lost, Murray . . ."

Sean made the save. "There's a map in my guidebook, De. I'll take it."

Instead of giving Sean his props, De whirled around and was all, "And what are you planning to wear?"

Just then the phone rang. Amber answered it.

"It was Geist," she announced when she hung up, "reminding us that we should take bathing suits, sunblock, and all our documentary equipment, because we're making a lot of stops along the way. There are places to swim, and there might be a seal sighting or something. And she said to tell you something about your brother Josh calling to give you the number of his hotel, Cher. Call her back if you want it."

Want Josh's number? As if! I elected to conveniently forget that part of the message and began uploading my backpack with necessities for the next day's voyage.

"Hana is a quaint village on the eastern end of the Maui," Chad was describing as we regrouped the next morning in the hotel lobby. Our guide was borderline Baldwin this A.M., having chucked his khakis in favor of Hilfiger shorts and a snug T-shirt, which amply displayed his defined cuts. I noticed that Miss Geist noticed, too.

"In and of itself," Chad was detailing, "Hana is no great shakes. But the Hana Highway is one of Maui's best-known tourist attractions. It's fifty miles of winding, narrow road with fifty-six one-lane bridges and over six hundred hairpin turns." He chuckled as he turned to Miss Geist. "I don't think you've got anything like it in Los Angeles."

"Excuse me, wouldn't it be more expedient to simply charter a helicopter and avoid the potentially injurious, not to mention arduous, faux freeway altogether?" Amber suggested.

"Going to Hana is about the journey, not the destination, Amber," Chad countered. "Wait till you guys see where we're going to stop. There are magnificent waterfalls, awesome arboretums, and black sand beaches," he described, distributing maps marked with scenic roadside inlets.

De scanned the map purposefully. "There, that's it. Nahiku," she declared. "That's where the beach house is."

Murray, Sean, Jesse, Amber, and I leaned over to see. De had pulled a red felt marker from her Coach bag and circled the town located right on the water. A squiggly road off the main highway led directly to it.

Awesome! Hooking De up with her clan was going to be massively cinchy. We did a group high-five as Chad admonished us, "We're caravaning, kids, so we must stay together. Follow me and Miss Geist. We'll be in the lead car. And make sure your gas tanks are full before we start. There are no gas stations along the way."

There were four Jeeps in the Bronson Alcott procession, and by the time we called a bellhop to load ours with De's ensembles and our documentary equipment, we ended up last in line. We were finally ready to depart, when suddenly we noticed Miss Geist running toward us, frantically waving her arms. She was wearing a full-out safari trousers ensemble replete with brimmed rattan hat, only on her it didn't so much say Banana Republic as forest ranger.

" 'Zup, Miss Geist?" I asked, poking my head out of the backseat. Our teacher appeared profoundly flustered.

"I'm going with you. We need an adult to bring up the rear." That was her explanation, but her body language spelled extreme discomfort. "Jesse, you go in the lead car, with Chad, Summer, Janet, and Ringo," she directed.

Jesse was severely unthrilled at being booted from our Jeep, but the look on Geist's face advised against protest.

He left that to De.

My main t.b., ballistic at the thought of our plans going awry, challenged our authority figure. "Travel with us? You can't!"

But Geist was fully determined. Squeezing into the front seat, she was all, "I'm sorry, Dionne. Move over."

Call me mental, but I didn't think Geist's change of travel plans had anything to do with needing to be the rear view authority figure or a premonition about our beach house sidebar. I'd bet my new Alaïa it had to do with Chad and her feeling vaguely uncomfortable around him.

De flashed panicked eyes at me. With my own body language, I tried for reassuring, reminding De that Geist was not only malleable but radically distracted. As we pulled out onto the road, I could only hope I was right.

The Hana Highway, as Chad had cautioned, was riddled with random zigs and zags, studded with those single-lane bridges, rising and dipping fully haphazardly. Sean had brought his guide book and instructed Murray, "It's the custom here to let the other vehicle have the right of way on the bridges, especially if the driver blinks his lights at you. Don't honk your horn. It's rude."

Murray totally took heed. But being brutally polite lost us valuable time. Which is why it didn't take us long to lose Chad and all the cars in our group ahead of us.

Miss Geist didn't seem to mind. Like, hello, she didn't seem to notice. She mostly stared out the window, wordless.

After traveling an hour or so, we decided to stop at the first place Chad had marked on the map, Puohokomoa Falls. It turned out to be a way decent attraction that made Niagara Falls seem overdone. These falls were smaller, but poetically idyllic, as was the tourist-addled pool it spilled into. I scanned for members of the Bronson Alcott posse, but my schoolmates must have done this and gone to the next attraction already. Meanwhile, Sean capably informed us that *Puohokomoa* translated as "valley of the chickens bursting into flight."

"My life is so much more complete for that knowledge," Amber replied sarcastically. "Can we, like, move on?"

We did, but not before a brief plunge into the boxed lunch the hotel had thoughtfully provided. De took the opportunity to dash into the rest room and switch ensembles in preparation for the historic meeting. She'd started out in a halter top and shorts but emerged from the changing room totally pushing the Tyra envelope in a long matte jersey dress with keyhole neckline.

I managed to convince Miss Geist, who didn't comment on De's wardrobe change, that she'd be more comfortable in the backseat with Amber and Sean, while I positioned myself next to De. That way, my main and I could scheme more efficiently.

We'd driven for another hour, winding past taro patches and furious foliage, when suddenly De yelped, "There! Stop! It's there—the turnoff for Nahiku." There was no sign indicating it, but De had been following the map mega-precisely. "Make a left, Murray," she instructed.

I spun around to check Miss Geist's reaction to De's outburst. She peered at me quizzically, and softly said, "Nahiku? I don't remember that as one of the stops."

"Actually, Miss Geist, it isn't," I concurred.

Okay, so I could have simply told our teacher that we'd heard about a monk seal sighting and wanted to check it out. But something said, Cher, Miss Geist is mired in her own silent crisis. Tell her the truth.

Before Amber could stop me, I explained, "This is the turnoff to the beach house that De's father's third ex-wife owns. Remember?"

Geist blinked. She seemed to be conjuring up the memory. "Oh, yes, I do remember now. That was the reason you wanted to come to Hawaii in the first place, wasn't it, Dionne?"

De flipped around in her seat and threw Geist a beseeching look.

"Would you mind, Miss Geist? It's right off the highway, as you can see." She pointed at the map, but Geist never glanced at it.

Our teacher just said, "Well, all right. But only for a short while. We'll just get to Hana a little later than the rest of our group."

My take? Geist was way ambivalent about catching up with Chad.

"Thank you, Miss Geist," De gushed, relieved. "You are such the best teacher. I will never forget this."

To Murray, De instructed, "Make a right."

Okay, so it's like that famous poem, "Things in the mirror are closer than they appear." When you're reading a map, it's the opposite. Things are never as close as they appear.

I mean, I'm no cartographer, but that squiggly road off the Hana Highway? Which ostensibly led to Nahiku? Hello, it could not have been over an hour's drive away. Yet, there we were, seventy-five minutes after Geist had given the turn-off go-ahead, and no beach house in sight. No beach either.

There was a small town, however.

De leaned over and hit the horn in an attempt to snag the attention of generic passersby.

Annoyed, Murray was all, "Stop it, woman. What are you doing?"

"Don't woman me, Murray. We are obviously not on the road to the beach house. We need to ask directions."

But Murray refused to brake. "We got directions, we don't need other directions. We're going the way you said—to the right. There's only one road, and it leads to the shore. It's just taking longer than we thought is all."

Amber piped up, "Excuse me, *right?* She said *left,* Murray. Like over an hour ago."

Sean leaped to Murray's defense. "What's up, Amber? De said right, and that's the way my man went. Stop trying to confuse the issue."

De and I pulled out the map and tried to remember which way she had, in fact, told Murray to go. And like, where we'd be if by some heinous twist of fate, he'd opted for the road, like, less traveled? Miss Geist tried to help by calling out street markers. But no one's map, neither ours nor Sean's, was that detailed.

And, hello, nowhere on any map did it indicate that like, the paved part of the road would end so brutally. But suddenly, like a Kate Moss crop top, it just did.

What was once pavement was now dirt and gravel, a rutted and bumpy path riddled with rocks and sagebrush. Which bizarrely, Murray took as a good sign. "Look, we ran out of road. The water's gotta be close by."

But in every direction we scanned, all we saw was more . . . land. An unhealthy shade of brown, dusty, dry land.

Luckily, we weren't alone. Another car was behind us. De yelled frantically, "Let's flag them down and ask for directions."

Only Murray went all mulish, taking it as some impingement on his Baldwinhood. He refused and only slowed to allow the car to pass us. Stubbornly, Murray insisted, "We don't need to ask directions. We're going the right way. I know it."

"No you don't. You don't know anything!" De cried.

Miss Geist entered the fray. "Sean, let's check your guidebook carefully. Maybe there's something helpful in it."

Sean pored over it and then tapped Murray on the shoulder. "Uh, bro? I think I know what happened. Maybe you'd better pull over."

Murray did as told. Sean explained, "I think we might've gone inland instead of toward the water. I mean, look in my book, it shows ranches here. And doesn't this scenery look more Ponderosa than *Baywatch* to you?"

Miss Geist agreed. "Sean's right."

Murray grumbled, "I don't get it. We went the right way. But, hey, I'm not gonna fight with all of you. De, just call Chandra and get directions from where we are."

"And where would that be, Murray?" De seethed. "At the intersection of a rock and a hard place? How are we going to tell them where we are?"

I reached for my cellular and my soothing tone. "What's their number, De? I'll call."

De snatched it away from me and punched in the digits, but all she got was more frustrated.

"It's not going through! It's, like, roaming. Murray, get us out of here. Turn around."

Amber brandished her cellular. "Hello? My phone is the newer model. I'll get through."

De dictated the digits, but Ambu-lame had no better luck. Disgustedly, she was all, "We are so off-the-beaten-tracking it. Make a U-ie, Murray."

"We can't," Murray countered.

"We *can't?* Says who?" De demanded.

"Mr. Gas Tank, that's who," Murray retorted, pointing at the gauge. It was pointing toward empty. "We don't have enough gas to get back to the main road. We're better off continuing in this direction and hoping we come to civilization."

And we sort of did, not fifteen minutes later.

Only it wasn't exactly the civilization Murray had in mind.

"Moo-oo, moo-oo." We heard the groaning sounds in the distance.

We didn't even have to play Name That Species. For just as we crested a ridge, we were greeted with a wholly unexpected sight. A herd of cows was totally milling about, taking up valuable roadway. They reminded me of the slackers at our school.

At least Sean was psyched. "Excellent! I was right! We are inland, by the ranches." He went to high-five Miss Geist, who actually smiled and high-fived him back.

Murray stopped the car. A contingent of brash bovines took that as a cue to lumber over for a better view. While most kept a respectful distance from the Jeep, one seemed especially taken with Amber and moved in perilously close.

"They think you're one of the herd, Amber," Sean snickered.

De actually broke out of her ballistic to giggle. "I think that one likes you."

Amber tried waving her new admirer away. "Ick! Get out of here! Get away from me!"

My take? What the cow heard was "And I like you, too."

It actually stuck its head in the car and nudged Amber, who started to scream and push it away, "It's slobbering on me! Go away! Drive, Murray!"

The disadvantages of an open-air Jeep were becoming apparent.

Even more so, ten minutes later. That's approximately when, without warning, the flash flood started. Torrents of overwrought raindrops viciously beat down on us. Not to mention washed out what semblance of road there was.

But like that famous saying "What else could go wrong?" it didn't really matter. Our Jeep started to sputter and slowly ground to a halt.

We'd run out of gas anyway.

Chapter 6

Okay, so we were vehicularly impaired and temporarily displaced.

"We're Fugees," Murray quipped, invoking the name of that famous group, slang for *refugees.*

His attempt at levity was so not met with equal goodwill. De was beyond nuclear. She continued to shout at him. "Why did you turn right? I said left!"

"If you knew how to read a map, we wouldn't be lost, woman!"

"Oh, so it's my fault? Because you refused to stop for directions, I'm not going to see my family! I'm never going anywhere with you again, Murray!"

"Don't worry, Miss Dionne. I'm never taking you anywhere again!" Murray barked.

As they bickered, Amber assigned more blame. "If it weren't for you two morons, I wouldn't be stuck in this nightmare! I'm calling Daddy to send a rescue helicopter!" Then she remembered that we were in a phone-free zone and pouted some more.

Sean poured over his book, now drenched. As if that would help us.

Miss Geist just sighed woefully, lost in inertia-ville.

I struggled to maintain composure. Once, on a faux spa encounter that turned into a nature experience, De and I learned to survive in the wild. We fished. We foraged. We kayaked and mountain climbed. We got an award.

Only that time, we weren't lost. But hello, once you've learned survival skills, they're furiously adaptable. It's like learning to ride a bike. Or steer a Jaguar. Or something. Whatever. My leadership skills were desperately needed.

I opted for inspirational. "There's no sense sitting in the car. We need to take charge of our destiny. I propose we snare our valuables and whatever supplies we can carry, and hike to the nearest town."

"Excuse me, who put you in charge, Sacajawea?" Amber, who thanks to the downpour, now resembled a drowned Afghan hound, groused.

Murray snapped at her, "You got a better idea?"

That's when Miss Geist sternly pulled it together. "Cher's right. We don't have a choice. Out of the car, everyone. Let's go. We've got to get to a phone. Alfonse will be worried sick if we don't return with the group."

Our teacher had spoken. Murray and Sean put the car in neutral and guided it off the muddy road so it wouldn't get accidentally sideswiped.

Although the punishing rainstorm had ended as

abruptly as it started, we were soaked beyond repair. Sticky, crabby, and sartorially inept for a hike, we still gathered our backpacks and the video camera and trudged forth bravely through the sludge. With each step, splotches of mud splashed up on my exposed calves. I might never be able to look at a mud bath the same way again.

We hadn't gotten very far before Amber started whining that her feet hurt. While none of us had worn hiking boots, she was the only one in Jil Sander stiletto-heeled sandals. Even I went empathy-centric, but I soon ran out of patience as she kept up a steady stream of complaints.

"I can feel my blood sugar falling! My throat is constricting. I need the facilities. This is so not in the Hawaii tourist brochures. I'm telling Daddy to sue for false advertising."

At least the late afternoon sun had started to dry us off. And although neither De nor I had thought to bring proper foraging tools, I wasn't bereft of emergency supplies.

"Evian, anyone?" I offered. There wasn't much left in the bottle, but my grateful trailmates each availed themselves of a sip. As Miss Geist handed me back the empty bottle, she looked so tragic. I knew she needed me to help her unburden. Since the two of us were a few paces in front of the others anyway, I went for it.

"You seem profoundly preoccupied," I said to our teacher. "It can help to share. I know that, okay, we're not your normal peer group, but it's like, 'If you can't be with the one you love, love the one you're with.' "

Invoking that famous ancestral folk song slogan was all it took. With a massive sigh, Geist spilled. "It's just that I wanted Alfonse to be more of an adventurer. To take more chances. He went around the other side of the mountain yesterday to prove to me that he could. And now look what happened."

Gently, I prodded, "And . . . what about Chad? Miss Geist, he was totally flirting with you."

"Was it that obvious? It's just that, for a crazy second, Chad seemed to be everything Alfonse isn't."

"Well, I admit he's folliclely enhanced and way knowledgeable in his field of expertise, but—"

"He's a snake, Cher," Miss Geist said bitterly. "This morning, the minute Alfonse's back was turned, he actually had the nerve to come on to me. What kind of man would do that? But I blame myself. Maybe I gave him mixed signals. Anyway, I had to get away from him."

"You did the right thing, Miss Geist," I said soothingly. "Because deep down you're really sprung on Alf—that is, Mr. Hall. Don't worry, we'll get through this roaming area soon and you'll be able to call him."

She smiled bravely. "I know we will, Cher."

After we'd trudged for what totally must have been miles, the flat, desert quality of our terrain gave way to woods. Though we followed a clearly marked path, it was choked with bushes, vines, and unidentifiable vegetation. Avoiding the low-flying branches and brambles sapped what was left of our energy.

Then, all at once, out of nowhere, a vision appeared. My makeup was already trashed from the rain, so I went ahead and rubbed my eyes to be sure it wasn't a mirage.

But Sean saw it, too. "Eureka! Civilization!" he shouted triumphantly.

Okay, so like, overstatement. Hello, it was . . . a fruit stand. A structurally indecisive shack implausibly situated in the middle of the woods.

But what it lacked in ambience, it totally made up for in inventory. Stocked with a massive profusion of bananas and pineapples, it was a furiously welcome sight. Best of all, there were two saleswomen.

"Hola, amigas!" Amber, about three continents off, rushed toward them and began to place her order. She actually asked which of the pineapples were ripest, and did any come cored?

The fruit stand employees' command of English was somewhat lacking, but they tried to be obliging, and offered us bananas and pineapple juice, which we gratefully accepted. They threw up their hands in confusion, though, when Amber tried to pay with her American Express gold card. Luckily, Murray had cash.

Miss Geist went into full-tilt charades in an effort to explain our plight, but alas, native Hawaiian seemed to be their mother tongue, and our teacher was vastly undereducated in it.

Sean wasn't. As our total hero stepped forth, his drenched book of translation in hand, we stood back in awe. Even Amber had to give Sean his props, as he capably asked directions to the nearest *aliloa*.

From what Sean explained later, the fruit stand women told us we'd gone all *mauka*, toward the mountains, instead of *makai,* toward the sea. Then they pointed to another path leading to the highway, which was, they assured us, near the sea.

"Mahalo," Sean had responded—Hawaiian for thank you.

Knowing we were on the right path provided just the burst of energy we needed. As we made our way through the thickets, every so often, we'd try our cellulars again, but tragically, we remained connection-challenged. It reminded me of trying to get on AOL.

"Did they say how long until we reached that *makai* thing?" De asked, concerned. "It's after seven and it's getting dark."

"If they did, the translation wasn't in my book," Sean admitted.

We soldiered on. Was it only yesterday that we'd actually complained about that micro jaunt up the hill? It now seemed like the equivalent of the bunny slope at the ski resort.

"My feet are so not improving," Amber was just reminding us about an hour later, when miraculously, we saw a clearing in the trees up ahead. We quickened our pace. As we got closer, we could see . . . no, not that *aliloa* highway thing, but a sparkling, pristine beach and the white-foamed shoreline of what totally had to be the ocean.

Okay, so that in and of itself didn't spell rescue, but the aura of a not immediately identifiable foodstuff was a fully positive sign. So was, as we got nearer, the sounds of music. Even if it was that Jurassic group the Beach Boys doing "Kokomo."

"Yo! Yo! Anyone there?" Murray shouted, sprinting ahead of us.

Like double eureka, there so totally was!

I surveyed the scene. A posse of furiously buff Gen-X types, three dudes and two dudettes, were hunched around a campfire on the beach, primitively roasting hot dogs on sticks. It was about 8:30 P.M., and by the light of the fire I could see they were deeply tanned. That and their ensembles gave them away: all five were comparably attired in flowing, midcalf shorts, reef sandals, and colorful Hawaiian short-sleeved shirts. Like at school? They'd so fit in with the boardies: transposed to the shores of Hawaii, they had to be such the surfers. And segue: A quintet of advertisement-laden surfboards was propped up by a log cabin, one of several in a beachy cul-de-sac formation nearby.

But if we were surprised to stumble upon the surfers, their reaction at seeing us bordered on shock: five mud-caked, designer-clad, vehicularly challenged Beverly Hills refugees and their teacher, emerging apparition-like from the woods behind them.

Wide-eyed, all five surfers whirled around and rushed over to greet us. One of the dudes blurted, "Man, you guys must have taken some wrong turn. Where did you come from?"

But before we could respond, another one was all, "Come on over, sit by the fire. You guys hungry? Thirsty? We got food."

Gratefully, we introduced ourselves to the band of surfers and accepted their hospitable offer of nourishment and use of the facilities. As we hunkered down on the beach by the campfire, only Amber inquired about a chaise longue.

We explained our tragic plight. While we were relieved to unburden, we were massively bummed to learn they were fully phone-challenged. Although their cabin had a phone, it wasn't turned on because they didn't exactly live here—they were only renting for the week. The other cabins were woefully unoccupied. The only working phone in the area was in the office of the gas station—already closed at this hour. As for our high-priced, high-tech mobile units? They were still function-impaired.

Miss Geist was buggin' but stoic. The rest of us were too tired to trip.

But hello, a true Betty is never so wiped out that her radar doesn't pick up the vibes from an especially significant studmuffin unexpectedly in her midst. The one in my personal midst had huge almond-shaped hazel eyes; straight, jet black hair that fringed his shirt collar; and a megawatt smile that lit up the night. His name, he told me, was Lee. And even though I was so not in top Betty form, I'm sure he appreciated my potential.

He seemed to be the leader, or at least the most verbal, of the pack, who'd introduced themselves as Chris, Don, Kelly, and Sue. They explained that they were on a break from the pro surfers' tour and only camped out here to practice for the week.

"The rip curls are flyin' here," Lee described, which I took to mean the waves were really, really righteous.

De didn't care about the waves. Mournfully, she was all, "Are we far from Nahiku?"

"Nahiku?" Chris echoed. "Whoa, that's all the way back up toward Hana on the eastern shore. That's where you were headed? I don't know how you managed it, but you must've cut through the middle of the island because you're on the south shore now."

"Like we totally zigged when we should have zagged?" I guessed.

"Totally," Lee confirmed, favoring me with a gentle smile.

On the upside, he explained, the entire island wasn't that big, and he and his friends knew their way around. They assured us that we were closer to De's ancestral beach house than we were to the Grand Hyatt Wailea.

Before we could initiate any plan to go anywhere, however, we needed to phone the hotel, reclaim our gas-deficient Jeep, and get some restorative rest. Alas, due to our condition and the late hour, our only option was to wait out the night and phone home first thing in the morning. Lee and his surfer friends were gracious hosts, offering us the full complement of those roadside signs: food, gas, lodging. Also hot showers and clean towels.

And, like, suddenly? Spending the night there seemed furiously choice.

Lodging turned out to be in their stylistically challenged three-room cabin. But after the trudge-fest we'd just endured, the Spelling mansion could not have been a more welcome sight. Okay, maybe, but only if the *Melrose Place* cast was visiting.

De, Amber, and I surveyed the micro-room we

would share for the night. It was fully bare, except for twin beds and a nubby pull-out couch. Attempting levity, I quipped, "Well, we did end up finding a beach house."

Only De's face, so tragic, stopped me from continuing.

I put my arm around her. "Don't worry, Dionne. It'll just take an extra day, but we'll get there. The main thing is, we're safe, we're together, we totally weathered adversity. And we're still basically on our way."

Amber, who'd settled on the couch, moaned. "Look at my foot. I need to soak it. I've got blisters. And my first callus."

"Not if you count attitude." De yawned, flopping backward on the bed.

Amber tried to respond but she must have been too zonked. By the time she opened her mouth, Sue and Kelly, who were sharing with Miss Geist, appeared in our doorway with three pairs of clean, if generic, pajamas, and robes all around, and bid us good night.

An hour and a hot shower later, De was in dreamland and Amber was snoring. Only I was still twisting and turning, sleep-challenged. I thought maybe the ocean air would make me drowsy, so I threw on the borrowed robe and tiptoed out of the cabin, careful not to let the screen door slam behind me. I'd only taken a few steps toward the water when I heard someone call my name.

"Uh, Cher? Is that you?"

Startled, I spun around. Lee had been sitting out on

the cabin's front porch, nursing an iced tea. I hadn't even seen him in the shadows.

"Is everything okay?" he asked, concerned.

"I couldn't sleep," I responded.

Lee gazed out to the sea. "The ocean air is soothing, isn't it? I'll take a walk with you, if you want—I mean, if it's all right."

I so wasn't dressed for a moonlight beach stroll with a Baldwin, but what choice did I have?

"So, you live near the ocean?" Lee asked as we strolled barefoot on the damp, grainy, tightly packed nighttime sand.

"More near the hills. What about you? I mean, when you're not here. Where are you from?"

"I *am* from here," Lee responded. "I'm a native. Grew up in Honolulu."

"Is surfing what you always dreamed of doing?"

"More like my destiny," Lee confirmed. "My dad was a surfer, and my mom hit the waves, too. It's Hawaii's native sport, you know."

"I bet you're ferocious at it," I said coyly, eyeing his sinewy upper body and strong legs. "I mean, didn't you mention something about going pro?"

"Going pro? Oh, you mean the pro surfers' circuit. Yeah, I'm on it, we all are. But . . . well, we're not all on it for the same reasons."

Curious, I stopped short to gaze up at Lee. His big, gentle eyes held mine, as the moonlight danced off his jet black hair.

"See, Cher, there's a lot of money to be made on the pro circuit. That's what most of them are after, chasing the big money prize of corporate sponsorship."

"But not you?" I said softly.

"Nah. That's not what it's about for me. Surfing is . . . I don't know if you can understand. But it's like, when you look out there and see the ocean rising in a wall of shimmering blue, curling over hollow space with its edge tipped in foam—man! It's like the most exciting feeling in the world. Riding that wave, sliding across its face on the front of a board—it's—it's bliss."

"That was majorly poetic," I gasped, entranced.

Lee continued, "This place where we are now? It's a surfer's haven. The best waves, curling up to fifteen feet, give you long, sliding rides. That's why whenever we're on break, we rent this cabin for the week and spend it practicing."

Lee stopped, suddenly awkward. "But what am I droning on about? Have you ever surfed?"

Okay, so like conceptually, surfing had never appealed to me. The outfits, for one thing, were tow up. Like call me when the Dolce & Gabbana line of surfwear debuts. Also, surfing entails full salt-water dousing. Which, hello, plays havoc with my skin, hair, and nails.

Still, I didn't want to lose favor with Lee, so I opted for honest-cute. "Does channel or Web surfing count?"

He threw his head back and laughed. "You're adorable, Cher. And sweet. Tell your boyfriend he's lucky to have you."

I couldn't believe it. Lee was fishing to find out if I had a hottie stashed away. I set him straight.

"I don't have a boyfriend, Lee. But does your

girlfriend know how poetic you are?" Like, you didn't have to get wet to fish.

Lee softly cupped my chin in his hand. Gently, he tilted my face up toward his. Just before our lips met, he murmured, "I don't have a girlfriend, Cher."

Chapter 7

It's amazing what a rejuvenating good night's sleep will do. Like, everyone woke fully chipper the next morning. But I was the only one actually humming, as I draped myself in a generic J. Crew-esque shorts outfit, compliments of Kelly. She and Sue had fully opened their wardrobe to us, since we couldn't possibly put back on the stiff, muddy ensembles we'd arrived in yesterday.

De, a quirky vision in baggy surfer shorts that clashed heinously with a Hawaiian shirt, eyed me suspiciously. "What's with the humming, Cher? You only hum when you're . . . Did I miss something last night?"

Since Amber, who'd scored one of Sue's more unfortunate "skort" outfits—a heinous hybrid of shorts and a skirt—was among us, I opted for vague. But my eyes twinkled when I answered, "Let's just say the night epilogued on a more positive note than it began."

I left De to ponder that as I followed the retro aroma of eggs, bacon, and toast that wafted from the kitchen—the kind of cholesta-fest that gives agita to nutritionists all over Beverly Hills. But as I headed toward breakfast, I felt a ping of nostalgia: Daddy will probably be gorging on just this in a few hours. Like when Cher's away, the lawyer will play.

"Morning, Cher," Lee said, winking slyly at me. Standing bare chested and barefoot at the stove, scrambling up eggs, he was brutally hot.

If Miss Geist and Lee's surfer crew had not been there, scarfing breakfast around a makeshift table, I would have said something more meaningful than "Mmm . . . smells tasty."

But I'm pretty sure Lee got my drift. His smile said so.

De and Amber followed me into the kitchen and settled themselves around the table next to Miss Geist, who looked especially jarring in one of Sue's knee-length surfer shorts outfits.

Attending to the task at hand, Lee was all, "How do you take your eggs, girls?"

Just then Murray and Sean sauntered in. One glance at De's surf shorts and Murray grinned wickedly. "Nice to see your face in the place. And don't you look—"

De held up a cautioning hand. "Don't go there, Murray."

To avert a Murray-De spat, Geist quickly cleared her throat and announced our ASAP agenda. "These young gentlemen"—she nodded at Don and Chris—

"have graciously offered to drive Murray and Sean back to the spot where we left our car. They'll bring a canister of gas. Meanwhile, Kelly, Sue, and I will go to the phone to call Alfonse—unless anyone else wants to join us?"

De was all, "I'm there. I have to call Chandra."

Amber dittoed, "I'm calling Daddy."

Since I didn't have anyone to call, I volunteered to stay at the cabin. With my hang-ten hottie, Lee.

Generously, Chris offered, "When we get back with your car, do you want us to guide you to Nahiku? Or take you back to your hotel? 'Cause we'd be glad to do either."

De flashed our teacher a beseeching look. "Please, Miss Geist. We've come this far. And like they said, we're much closer to the beach house than the hotel. Please, can we go there first?"

Geist sighed. "I have to talk to Mr. Hall. We'll see, Dionne."

After everyone had left, Lee said casually, "Miss Geist mentioned that you were doing a documentary on endangered species when you got lost." He was leaning back against the stove, sipping a mug of steaming coffee.

I nodded. "That's the reason—well, it's one reason we came on this trip. But so far we've only spied one pod of humpbacks. And, well, it's sort of complicated, but we didn't even end up documenting it on tape."

Lee stroked his chin. "Any chance your video camera is here?"

That was one of the few things we hadn't left in the

car. "It's probably in the room Murray slept in. Why?"

"Well," he said, resting his coffee cup on the counter, "actually, we're not too far from a coastal nature trail where green sea turtles have been known to come ashore and hatch their eggs. It's not a bad place to spot whales, either. It's probably gonna be a few hours until your friends come back with the car. If you're game, we could take the camera and hike there. Who knows? Maybe you'll get lucky."

While the word "hike" did so not connote pleasure, the idea of spending the morning with Lee more than made up for it. I dashed into Murray's room to fetch the endangered species cam.

Lee chivalrously shlepped the video camera as he led me past where the beach ended to a hilly trail that snaked the shoreline. With his free hand, he held mine so I didn't slip on the rocky parts. On our left, the aquamarine ocean sparkled in the sunlight as gentle waves lapped the pebbly shore. On our right, the terrain was dry and crusty, brutally unlike anything I'd seen before, either in Hawaii, Beverly Hills, New York, or Paris. I pointed to a bunch of huge spiny green orbs that dotted the landscape. "The flora and fauna here are way Koosh ball," I noted.

Lee's eyes twinkled. "That's a silversword, Cher, a plant unique to Hawaii."

Though Lee didn't know if it was an endangered foliage species, I decided to videotape it for that local color thing. I was sure that's what Murray would have wanted me to do.

"This is totally noble of you, Lee," I acknowledged

as we walked along. "Doing this favor for me. I mean, for us. I mean, all of your friends. Like, before last night, you didn't even know us."

Lee shrugged. "No biggie, Cher."

"Hello, it was deeply big. Your crew magnanimously forfeited valuable surfing time," I protested. "It's a massive favor."

"Not to us, it isn't. It's just aloha, that's all."

"Aloha?" I echoed. "As in, that's your way of saying hello?"

Lee laughed. "That's the mainlanders' touristy definition. To native Hawaiians, it's more than just a word. It's sort of the code we live by."

As Lee further explained, I found out that aloha is way conceptually diverse. "Aloha means doing good—and not only to repay people who've been proper to us. Aloha tells us to welcome the stranger and seek the good in him or, uh, her. A person who has the spirit of aloha shows love even when the love is not returned. It's sort of our version of the golden rule. The basic concept of our culture is sharing."

"I so believe in that, too!" I enthused. "Like, De and I totally pledge to share our savvy with others less fortunate."

"Then I'd say we have a lot in common, Cher." Lee grinned at me.

When we came to a rock formation atop a small hill, Lee stopped, perched, and motioned for me to sit down next to him. He pointed to the shore. "This is it—the spot where I once saw a green sea turtle come ashore to lay its eggs."

As if on cue, the sweetest—albeit slimy—sea creature emerged from the ocean and waddled up on shore not three feet from our rocky perch. Okay, so like I'm no mammal maven, but it didn't look like a turtle to me. It had flapper-like fins, plus a noticeable lack of shell. And, segue, it was big.

A surprised grin spread across Lee's studly visage. "Ssshh." He held his finger up to his lips. "It's a monk seal. Let's not disturb it." Then he handed me the camera, indicating that videotaping would be okay.

Through the lens, I saw a furiously sweet-faced, blubber-bellied seal, flapping contentedly on the beach. I hit the Record button. In a totally unrehearsed performance, the seal rolled over, fully coating itself in sand. "That's so adorable!" I burbled, taping away.

Lee started to explain about monk seals, but I stopped him. "Wait."

I fished in the camera bag for the microphone that attaches to the camera and plugged it in.

"Would you mind talking into this?" I was sure our erstwhile narrator, Amber, wouldn't mind ceding the spotlight. Actually, I was sure she would, which made it all the more gratifying. But hello—opportunity was totally knocking, or flapping, and we'd be remiss if we didn't do our docu-duty.

Lee flashed a gleaming white dental display, took the microphone from me, and spoke into it.

"This is a Hawaiian monk seal, found no other place on earth. Legend says it's Hawaii's first mammal, and it is the first to be nearly annihilated by hunters, explorers, and seamen. It is now protected, and we've got over a thousand populating the Hawaiian Islands National Wildlife Refuge. The monk seal loves sandy beaches and shallow water. And"—Lee paused—"as long as I've got the microphone, just let me say that I think Cher is the sweetest babe I've met in a long time and—"

Quickly, I put my hand over the microphone. "That was, uh, really proper, Lee, but a little off topic, don't you think?"

He grinned. "Off topic, but very much on my mind."

I matched his smile with one of mine. "I'm rewinding the tape. Let's finish this first, okay?"

"You're right, Cher." He cleared his throat. "Okay, monk seals, sea turtles, humpback whales, and their food resources are under constant threat from whalers and pollution."

Lee explained that he and his surfer buds were extra sensitive to pollution, especially gross beach invaders like raw sewage. Duh, it only made sense. Surfers spent prodigious time in the ocean.

"But pollution isn't the only enemy," Lee continued. "Endangered animals are also threatened by greedy developers looking to build luxury hotels."

I flashed on the one we were staying at and felt a stab of guilt. I resolved to have Janet talk to her father. All at once, between what I was videotaping and what Lee was saying, I realized the total importance of what we'd come to document. Miss Geist had nailed it: these species did need protecting.

Suddenly, Lee leaped up and pointed toward the horizon. "Look out there, Cher. I just saw something. I bet it's a whale."

I trained the video camera out to sea, and what came into the viewfinder was like an entire whale posse. Lee was all, "Aren't they something? Look at them, spy-hopping and spouting. I've seen thousands, and they never cease to amaze me."

Lee was right. The humpbacks were having a fluking fiesta. But something else struck me as I videotaped away. Like no one whale was trying to dominate or push the others away. I realized that Lee and his friends had mastered that cooperation thing, too. Even without amenities, they lived in righteous harmony.

I finished taping, and Lee and I held hands and looked out at the water. Quietly, I shared my observations with him.

"That's also part of the Hawaiian culture, Cher. Here wealth is measured not by what you have, but by how you feel."

Right then I felt completely fulfilled—the same effect a furious shopping spree has on me. Or being next to a furious hottie.

Lee put his arm around me and I snuggled up close to him. Carefully, I put the camera down and we kissed.

By the time we returned to the cabin, I was massively pumped. I'd gotten amazing footage and learned so much about aloha. And about Lee. I couldn't wait to tell my t.b.'s. As it turned out, our female faction was back already. Miss Geist, De, Amber, Kelly, and Sue were all out on the porch, sipping mineral water and gorging on grapes and pineapple slices. I intuited that all was well back at the hotel.

Miss Geist filled me in. "Thankfully, Alfonse is fine.

His foot is healing." Only it turned out that when all the other Jeeps returned from Hana without us, Mr. Hall was such the worrywart, he had sent the National Guard to look for us.

I turned to De. "And how did your call go, girlfriend?"

De lit up. "Stellar, Cher. Chandra still wants me—actually all of us, now that she knows the situation—to come and stay for as long as we can."

Miss Geist jumped in. "I explained about Dionne's relatives to Alfonse, and he agreed that we should go to the beach house first. I'll call him again from there. But"—she raised a cautioning finger—"we're not staying overnight or anything. Just long enough for Dionne to see her family."

"And speaking of family"—I gestured toward Amber—"what did Daddy tell Princess?"

Amber snorted and leaned back on her porch chair. "He said I have no case to file a lawsuit against the tourist bureau because we went off the road."

Lee, standing a few feet away from us, gazed longingly at the ocean.

"I bet you can't wait to get out there," I said empathetically, sidling up to him.

Lee tilted his head and gave me a curious smile. "I just got an idea. Since Murray and Sean aren't back with the car yet anyway, and the waves are pretty tame today, why not take a ride with me? You game?"

It was time to own up to the unembellished truth. "I've never surfed, Lee."

"I know that, Cher. Don't worry, we'll tandem surf. You and me together, on one board. Just for a little while. I want you get the feel of it, the rush of riding a wave. Then you'll understand why it means so much to me."

Lee was being such the sharing soul. How could I turn him down?

Tentatively, I ventured, "I guess I could try to conquer the waves."

Lee admonished, "The secret of surfing isn't about conquering the ocean. Surfing is flowing with the ocean."

Flowing with Lee was pretty much my motivation. I retreated into the cabin with Kelly, who offered to lend me one of her bathing suits. De followed me in. When Kelly was out of earshot, my main was all, "So what's the deal with you and the hang-ten hottie?"

"De, he's amazing! He's the beach Baldwin I came to find. He's buff, he cooks, he's furiously awash in the spirit of aloha, he's poetic—he's such the prince of tides."

"Slow down, Streisand. Maybe Lee is all that, but going surfing with him? Earth to Cher: you don't surf. I mean, unless you count channel—"

"Tscha, De! It's tandem surfing. Lee's too much the gentleman to set me adrift on a surfboard unchaperoned."

De was fretting. "I still don't think this is a good idea, Cher. Coordination, when it's not related to ensembles, has never been your strong suit."

Speaking of strong suits, the one Kelly had lent me was lamentably lame. Still, I slipped into it and assuaged De's fears. "Chill, girlfriend, it's totally safe."

De wasn't the only one concerned about my surf excursion. Miss Geist slid into the fret zone once

Amber tattled, "Cher has never surfed." It took Lee and me fully moments to assure her I'd be fine. Still, our teacher made us promise, only one wave, or fifteen minutes, whichever came first.

Lee snagged his surfboard from the side of the cabin. It was white but radiantly riddled with swatches of advertisements and slogans. The one I thumbs-upped read, "Save the whales. Harpoon a jet ski."

I followed him down to the shore.

"Okay," Lee said, turning to me as we tiptoed into the water, "This is how we do it. We'll walk the board out a few feet, then straddle it. I'll sit behind you. When I signal, we stand up on the board at the same time. Don't be nervous, I'll hold on to you."

I wasn't nervous at all. Being with Lee was way calming. The water was calm, too, and warmer than I thought it might be. As Lee instructed, we sat together, straddling the surfboard, and he began to paddle us farther out. After we'd ventured a few feet, Lee pointed toward the horizon, where a white-capped, petite-size wave seemed to be forming.

"See that wave out there? That one's ours. We'll start getting into position now. Stand up with me."

Gingerly, I swung one foot up and positioned it on the center of the board. Then I dittoed with the other one. I felt a little wobbly getting up, but Lee held me tight around the waist. Almost immediately, I started to slip, but Lee righted me. He demonstrated how to bend my knees and angle my arms out. The position felt unnatural. It reminded me of that classic movie, when the Karate Kid did that crane stance thing.

Suddenly, Lee whooped, "Here comes the wave, Cher. Get ready!"

And I was . . . getting ready, that is. Except right at that moment, out of the corner of my eye, I spotted a pod of humpback whales in the distance, just starting to breach.

Majorly psyched, I spun around to point at them. "Lee! Over there! More whales!"

His cry of "Don't move, Cher! You'll tip the board over!" was woefully tardy. I'd already stepped forward to get a better view. Suddenly, I felt this totally overwhelming sensation of plunging forward. The last thing I heard was a loud *thwack!*

And then everything went black.

Chapter 8

"Wake up, Cher!"

"Are you all right?"

"Oh no! She's hurt!"

I blinked. Above me, a cluster of generics was peering down. I had no clue who they were, but their voices betrayed frenzied anxiety. I was all wet and sticky from the sand glued to my back. And post-script: my head hurt.

A vivacious dark-haired, hazel-eyed Betty in a glaringly clashing shorts and shirt outfit seemed the most bugged. She knelt down beside me and grasped my arm.

"Cher! Are you all right?"

A flaming red-headed Monet, in an even more ridiculous ensemble, broke in. "She's not bleeding. She's conscious. I'll see if she's all right. Cher—insult me. Or if you're verbally impaired, at least get up."

"No, don't move her!" shouted a brutally hot, dark-haired Baldwin, who was kneeling on my other side. Like me, he was dripping wet. "She might need CPR. Clear away. Cher, say something! Can you speak?"

I blinked again. Why are they calling me Cher? Like, they think that's my name? Hello! My name is—is—it's—uh—

I bolted upright and frantically scanned my environs. I was on a beach. There was a cabin not far away. Hovering around me were those two unfortunately attired Bettys and one totally terrified Baldwin. Three others, including an older woman, were rushing toward us from the cabin.

Who were these randoms? Where was I? Images blurred together in my mind. I tried turning them, kaleidoscope-like, hoping that one of the mosaics would arrange itself into some sort of sense. But nothing did. I blinked again.

"She's sitting up!" the redhead declared, stating the obvious.

"Cher, can you speak?" the brunette cried anxiously.

"I think so," I whispered, peering at her intently. "Who are you?"

Like her eyes totally rolled back in her head just before she passed out.

Later I sat in the cabin amid these strangers and tried to think. My heart was pounding, and although I'd dried off from the ocean water, I was sweating profusely. Meanwhile, furious discussion swirled around me. I'd been able to walk unassisted, and except for that headache, nothing really hurt. I didn't think any bones were broken, as I assured this massively anxious assemblage.

The older woman, decked out in wrinkled safari garb that had seen better days, instructed the dude, "Tell us exactly what happened, Lee."

He answered her but faced me, his eyes filled with worry. "Cher and I were tandem surfing on my board. Everything was fine. The waves were gentle. I mean, I wouldn't have taken her out if they weren't. You've got to believe that, Miss Geist."

Miss Geist. What a weird name.

The Miss Geist person assured the Lee person she fully believed him.

He continued. "Cher spotted a humpback pod and shifted her position on the board. I tried to stop her, but she was so thrilled to see the whales, she threw us off balance and we wiped out. The surfboard hit her on the head."

Miss Geist looked at me with such brutal concern, I wondered if she was my mother.

"Are you sure nothing hurts you, Cher?" she asked again.

I nodded. "I'm pain free . . . I just can't remember anything."

The redheaded girl shrugged her shoulders. "She got hit in the head with a surfboard, and now she's got amnesia. Leave it to Cher to star in her very own cheesy soap opera."

I wondered why that girl was so hostile. I turned to the other girl, the one who'd passed out on the beach. She seemed fully revived. She walked over to me and put her arm around me.

"You're Cher," she said softly. "and we're your t.b.'s. I'm De. She's Amber. You *have* to know us, Cher."

"T.b.'s?" I questioned. "Isn't that some kind of disease?"

The look on De's face went into horror overdrive. "No, Cher. T.b. stands for true blue. As in true blue friends."

I gulped and faced Miss Geist. "Okay, so I'm sure this is a really lame question, but . . . by any chance . . . are you my mother?"

A tear totally came to her eye as she rushed up to me and put her arm around my other shoulder. "No, dear, I'm not. I'm your social studies teacher."

Then she explained that we were on a school field trip documenting endangered species in Hawaii—apparently the whole thing had been my idea—except it went furiously awry when we ventured off the road, got lost, ran out of gas, and ended up here. We were, in fact, on our way to being rescued when this heinous wipe-out thing happened.

I racked my brain. I blinked again. I stared at Miss Geist. Then at the Betty called De. And then at the one called Amber. Something would make me remember.

The dark-haired dude, Lee, knelt in front of me, his voice choked with emotion. "Cher, I am so sorry."

"Are you on the field trip, too?" I asked.

He shook his head and explained that he was one of the surfers who'd taken us in. Call me mental, but I had a sense there was something more between us.

I was about to ask, when the screen door of the cabin swung open and four significantly studly dudes appeared.

"Murray!" De shrieked, jumping up and throwing her arms around him. "Cher had an accident," she cried, "and now she can't—she's—"

"An amnesiac!" Amber interjected loudly. She sounded delighted. Like, what had I ever done to her?

Murray spun around. So did the other three. Concern flooded Murray's eyes. "What happened?"

De was all, "It was a surfing snafu."

Murray gasped. "Surfing? Cher don't surf. Unless you count channel—"

De cried, "We know! We've got to get to the beach house. Cher needs the foremost in medical attention, stat!"

Geist asked Lee, "Is there a hospital closer than that beach house?"

Lee shook his head. "There's a small medical center on the Hana Highway, but the closest actual hospital is in Wailuku. You're much nearer to the beach house. At least you can call for help from there."

De broke in excitedly. "I just remembered! One of Chandra's other exes is a doctor. I bet he's there! We so have no time. Let's go!"

The beach house? Weren't we already at a beach house? The confusion was overwhelming. Still, I had no choice but to ride it out, as it were. These strangers seemed fully committed to my health and welfare. Whoever I was.

After packing up what De and Amber assured me

were my belongings, I got into the back of a convertible Jeep, between Miss Geist and Sean, someone else I supposedly knew well. Murray drove, following a Dakota Sport pickup truck, in which Lee and one of his surfer friends, Chris, would lead us to the beach house.

De explained we were going to see relatives of hers she hadn't interfaced with in a long time. Including, she mentioned casually, her father. Okay, so I found that strange. But based on my current circumstance—what wasn't weird?

Along the way, I paid close attention to the terrain, hoping that something in the scenery would jog my memory. Suddenly, I saw a familiar sight. "Look, over there! Silversword plants!" I exclaimed, pointing out a patch of furious foliage. "They're native to Hawaii."

Everyone—including Murray, who hit the brake—whirled around to face me. "How did you know that, Cher?"

Tragically, I had no clue. I sighed, and we continued.

About a half hour had passed when the pickup turned off the main road and onto a winding, unpaved driveway. We followed. In the distance, I could see the ocean, and as we got closer, a huge, gleaming structure rose from the sand. It was way more majestic than the one we'd just come from. All bleached wood and glass, its vaulted ceilings pointed toward the late afternoon sky.

"There it is!" De yelled, bouncing excitedly in her seat, "Chandra's beach house! We're so here! We're finally here!"

The beach house was fully encircled by a wrap-around deck, which, as we got closer, I could see was the locale of a bodacious fiesta in full swing. Furiously well-attired people were doing laps around the deck, some balancing plates of food, others holding drinks. Brutal bantering proliferated. Even from our car, we could discern several high-voltage arguments in full effect.

Murray pulled up next to the steps leading to the deck. De immediately unsnapped her seat belt, flung open the door, and ran up the stairs, screaming, "Daddy! Daddy!"

An elegant advanced-age dude, wearing a stylish white linen sports jacket, separated himself from the crowd and bolted over to the top of the steps. As soon as he reached De, he threw his arms around her, shouting, "Dionne! You made it!"

But before he could say anything else, De was all, "Cher had an accident! She has amnesia."

"An accident? Amnesia? Where is she?" De's father gripped the railing and peered down at our car, which we'd all started alighting from. I heard him say, "Wait, Chandra's—uh—another of her ex-husbands—Arthur—is a doctor. I'll get him."

But before he could fish the physician from the fractious crowd, a spectacularly high-glam woman appeared at his side. She had to be the Chandra person De had told me all about on the drive over here.

Draped in an excellent nearly sheer off-white pants suit—and like I have no idea how I know this, but the word *Armani* sprang to mind—she shouted above the din, "Dionne! Darling! I am so tickled you actually made it." She kissed the air around De when De's dad interrupted to explain about me. Chandra whirled around to peer down at me. Then she was all, "Edward, do you really think Arthur could be of help? He's a dermatologist, darling."

Even though we had yet to be invited up, Miss Geist could hold back no longer. The social studies teacher bolted up the stairs in search of a phone. She couldn't wait another second, she explained, to call someone named Alfonse. Murray, Sean, Amber, and I looked at one another but refrained from following, waiting for further instructions from De.

Before we got any, Lee appeared at my side. He took my hand and led me a few feet away from the others. "I think I should go. I guess . . . well, it looks like you're in good hands here. Adult hands, at least. They've got working phones and— Oh, Cher, I am so sorry. I can't believe this happened."

I reached up to caress his smooth cheek. "I wish I knew what to say. Lee? Are we—is there something between us? I mean, it's okay if there isn't, I'm just—" Suddenly I had to laugh. This whole scene was massively surreal. Like, it mattered if this Lee and I were together? I didn't even know who I was!

Lee closed his eyes and encircled me in his arms. Pulling me tightly to his chest, he kissed the top of my head. "I know you don't remember—yet. But you have to believe me. You're special, Cher. You're warm and sweet and caring—and incredibly beautiful. There could have been something between us, but the truth is, we only met yesterday. And now this has happened, and it's all my fault."

He sounded so wigged, I just had to comfort him. "It's okay, Lee. I mean, I'll recoup my memory. Somehow. And even though I don't remember what happened, like, I know it couldn't have been your fault."

Lee blinked back a tear. "I'm gonna go, Cher. I'll call your hotel tomorrow to check on you. 'Bye." With that, he released me, dashed back to his friend waiting in the pickup truck, and drove away.

"Cher! Get Cher!"

It took a moment before I realized who De was calling for. From up on the deck, she gestured to me, Murray, Sean, and Amber. "Come up! All of you! There's a doctor here."

Instinctively, Murray and Sean rushed to my side to help me up the steps. I waved them away. "It's okay, guys, I can walk. I just can't remember."

De ushered me through the throng. Murray, Sean, and Amber tagged along. As De's ranting relatives paused just long enough to eyeball us, I couldn't help noticing the island styling that proliferated: I counted three Badgley Mischkas, at least two clean minimalist interpretations of Sonia Rykiel's featherweight sweater knits, several women in strapless tube tops with pull-on leggings. Grievously, I fully comprehended the irony in recognizing designer names but not my own. Like, isn't it ironic? Someone should write a song about that.

De, her father, and Chandra escorted me into an architecturally statuesque great room dominated by a meandering leather sectional. They introduced me to Arthur, the token family physician, who rose to greet me. With a totally tentative smile, he was all, "Sit down, Cher. It *is* Cher, isn't it?"

Before I could say, hello—that's what I'd like to know, he caught himself. "Oh, how silly of me. Sorry."

As I positioned myself on the couch, De hung by me, wringing her hands. I wondered why she hadn't changed into something a little more sartorially correct for her family reunion. I had noticed her monogrammed suitcases in the back of our Jeep. But De's preoccupation with me was all-consuming. She was all, "Arthur, can you help her?"

Arthur, all wiry and raisined from the sun, which struck me as odd for like, a skin doctor, was all, "Dionne—you're Dionne, right? The daughter of my ex-wife's husband just before me? Or was it after me? Well, I guess it doesn't matter. You do know, dear, that amnesia's not my specialty. I can check her reflexes and rule out certain injuries, but she might have suffered a concussion."

De was all, "Just do what you can, okay? Miss Geist's calling for backup."

With that, Arthur extracted a penlike flashlight and, leaning over me, shined it in my eyes. Then he tapped my knees with another blunt instrument. He asked me to demonstrate walking in a straight line while holding my arms out to the sides, and then again with my arms in front.

Sean, the joker in the bunch, couldn't contain himself. "Is this a sobriety test? 'Cause I can vouch for her—"

"Squash it, Sean!" De warned. "This is no time for lame jokes." Then she turned to Arthur. "Well?"

Arthur shrugged. "Physically, she seems fine. I noticed a surface bruise on her head, but otherwise she's okay—no blurry vision, her reflexes are fine. I can't be sure, but from what you've told me, my best guess is temporary amnesia."

Chandra was all, "Still, darling, shouldn't we get her to a hospital?"

Just then Miss Geist came bounding into the room, breathing rapidly and fluttering her hands around. She caught her breath and announced, "I just spoke to Alfonse. He's coming to get us. But first he's calling Mr. Horowitz and then he's contacting Josh and bringing him along, so it'll take a while until they get here."

De's eyes widened. *"Josh* is coming?"

Geist turned to her. "Well, yes, Dionne. Mr. Horowitz left strict instructions that in case of emergency, after calling him, we're to contact Josh, since he happens to be here this week. And even though Cher appears to be physically okay, I'd certainly characterize this as an emergency."

"Uh, time out," I interrupted. "Who's Mr. Horowitz? And who's this emergency-contact Josh person?"

Miss Geist's eyes welled up again. All the air seemed to go out of her as she sank onto the couch next to me. De was on the other side: they took turns explaining those two familial relationships to me. Nothing sounded familiar. I felt like such a tard.

De's dad, who'd hung by silently observing us,

finally said, "Look, it'll be a while until they get here. Why don't you all come outside, relax on the deck, and have some refreshments? The sunset over Maui is magnificent; maybe you haven't missed it yet."

Amber and Sean didn't have to be asked twice. They bolted out of the room. Murray, who was holding a video camera, enthused, "I'll get a shot of the sunset!"

When De and I started to follow, her dad sidled up to her. "This is terrible about Cher, but I am glad you're here, Dionne. I've missed you."

De flashed a smile—the first one I'd seen since I met her. That is, since I remember meeting her. I wondered if that Mr. Horowitz person brought such bodacious smiles to my lips.

I felt that I should probably give De and her dad some space, so I quickened my pace to catch up to Murray, Sean, and Amber.

De grabbed my elbow. "As if! Cher, you are fully not leaving my side."

Outside on the deck, Chandra and De's dad took De around to meet her relatives, and I tagged along. As I hung with them, I intuited that De's dad, vibrantly dashing and independently wealthy, was a quasi-retiree. His peripatetic nature—not to mention his marriages—often made visitations with De fully brief and haphazard. Still, right now, his adoration of De was in full effect. He kept telling her how proud he was of her, as he introduced her around. Which is why De so needed this interlude.

I also observed and applauded the stellar ensembles represented, not to mention the bodacious baubles adorning random necks, wrists, and fingers. I was less impressed with the personalities. Nearly all the sound bite soupçons I overheard were majorly combative.

De's clan appeared to be such the combustible crew.

At the first opportunity, I took De aside and asked what all the squabbling was about. De explained that Chandra's stepdaughter was engaged—the raison d'être for the fiesta—ergo, the usual pre-nup and wedding plans contretemps.

"That's what they're arguing about? Wedding plans—and planning for the breakup before the nuptials?"

De arched her eyebrows. I surmised that I wasn't supposed to be surprised by that. "Like, duh, Cher . . ." she trailed off. "Forget it. Let's upload some nutritional supplements."

As if on cue, an hors d'oeuvre–bearing butler approached, and we snagged some mini salmon bites and sushi bits. Off in a corner of the deck, I noticed Sean, Murray, and Miss Geist lounging in a conversation pit of luxe chaise longues. Amber had fallen asleep and was snoring loudly. Murray was taping her.

As we went to join them, someone tapped De on the shoulder. She began an animated interface, and I left her there.

I planted myself on a lounge chair next to Miss Geist and surveyed. I could see that Dionne was totally bonding with her extended family. Other people kept coming up to her, and with each new close kiss encounter, she lit up with delight.

Suddenly, I felt a surge of happiness for her. And that's how I knew that Dionne and I probably were—what had De called us?—t.b.'s. True blues. As I leaned back on the chaise longue, I eagerly awaited more true stuff to come to me. Would it?

Chapter 9

"Where is she? Is she all right?"

I must have dozed off, because those words seemed to be coming at me from an echo chamber. Slowly, I opened my eyes. A significantly attractive hottie with dark wavy hair was rushing toward me.

Murray jumped up and cried, "Josh, man, you made it!"

The Josh person's eyes, a sparkling shade of blue, clouded with concern when he focused on me. I bolted up from the chaise. I don't know why, but I rushed into his arms. He smelled fully familiar.

I heard De gasp, "I'm plotzing. She must be in really bad shape. She never lets him get that close to her."

Oops. Had I just gone all abnormal? Whatever. Besides, I wasn't the only hugger or huggee standing on the deck of the beach house. Miss Geist had buried her head in the wiry arms of a folliclely deprived, vertically and sartorially challenged older dude, whose left foot was mummified in bandages.

I surmised he was the Alfonse of her conversations. And even though I didn't remember ever seeing him before? Snap—clearly, these two were true soul mates.

When Alfonse finally unclasped Miss Geist, he patiently explained to me that he was Mr. Hall, my literature teacher. In a thin, nasal, yet strangely comforting timbre, he explained that he'd tried contacting Mr. Horowitz, my father, in various places—at his law office, at home, and via his pager—but the best he'd been able to do was leave word and wait for a return call.

"I didn't want to unnecessarily alarm your father, Cher, so I left a message saying we had a problem, but that you're physically okay. That's accurate, isn't it?" Hopefully, he regarded me.

Josh shook his head. "It's not like Mel not to call back, unless, of course, he was called away at the last minute and is in transit or something. He is in the middle of a volatile case. He said he might have to bail for New York at a moment's notice."

Mr. Hall reached up to squeeze Josh's shoulder reassuringly. "I'm sure Mr. Horowitz will call back any minute. It wouldn't surprise me if there was a message from him by the time we get back to the hotel. Which, I suggest we do posthaste."

Miss Geist agreed. "Dionne, why don't you say your good-byes to your family so we can get going?"

* * *

I rode back with Josh and my teachers in a van-and-driver combo apparently provided by the hotel; the rest of our crew took the Jeep. All along the way, Josh kept quizzing me and Miss Geist. I must have heard "What happened *exactly?*" and "You can't remember *anything?*" like, one hundred times, followed by exhaustive exhaling and long explanation redials. Josh seemed monumentally weirded out by what Mel was going to say when he found out.

As soon as we got back, we rushed to the hotel lobby—well, Mr. Hall sort of limped—only, tragically, my dad had not returned any of the messages.

"Well, that's it. I'm not waiting!" Josh abruptly declared. "I'm taking her to a hospital to be checked out." He stormed up to the concierge desk, demanding directions to the nearest full-service hospital.

Miss Geist bolted after him. "Josh, wait. Look, dear, I know you have the best intentions, but you don't have the authority to do that."

Josh turned on his heel and went ballistic. "Authority? What if she's bleeding internally or something? Look, Mel put me in charge, and I know what he'd want me to do."

Gently, Geist said, "Josh, legally, Mr. Hall and I are in charge. You're only nineteen. In the absence of Cher's father, we make the decisions."

I sighed and tried to break into the fray. "Look, I'm basically fine. Even the headache's gone. I'm just, uh, momentarily detail-deficient."

They all ignored me. Josh looked fierce, as if he was about to go all postal again, when Mr. Hall said calmingly, "However, I'm sure we all agree it's prudent for Cher to be evaluated. I'll get the release forms from our room, and we'll all go to the hospital."

De insisted on coming with us. Murray lobbied to come too, but Hall and Geist rebuffed the offer, sending him, Amber, and Sean back to their rooms.

I felt brutally out of control. And severely unthrilled. Just because I was memory-challenged didn't mean they could treat me like I was invisible. And like, I don't know why? But it totally felt irregular for other people to make decisions for me.

I glanced at my watch as we arrived at Maui Memorial Hospital: it was 1:27 A.M. I couldn't help noticing that I was wearing a golden Movado timepiece: I seemed to have excellent taste in accessories. I would have liked to pursue that train of thought with De, but tragically, current circumstances weren't conducive to a fashion discussion.

In fact, for like the next several hours, I was such the amoeba under the microscope. First, there was the interrogation—after Josh produced all sorts of health insurance forms and rider-charged release forms, which apparently my father had provided him with just in case. Okay, so I couldn't remember this Mel person? But a mental picture of a way overprotective type was forming.

Then came the poking and prodding by a gamut of generic medical types. I would have been profoundly wigged, but De stayed by my side faithfully. When I shot her a grateful look, she was all, "Duh, Cher, you would do this for me, instinctively."

By the time the tests were complete, it was like the next day. And all that came out of it? Hello, the derma-diagnosis ruled: "Temporary amnesia."

While no one could predict when, or how, I'd get my memory back, like those same four out of five doctors who recommend Bayer, fully believed that eventually I totally would. And segue: other than being detail-deficient, I was in chronic shape. Even my cholesterol was low.

Every so often, Josh and my teachers attempted phone or pager contact with my father, but to no avail. While the hospital graciously offered to extend further services, my teachers nixed that idea. The decision was to return to the hotel, wait to hear from Mel—and get some sleep.

I was massively grateful to find I was sharing a room with Dionne. Like, after all she'd done for me, I knew this Betty had my foremost interests at heart. I wasn't so sure about that Amber person, but she was in the room, too. Accessorized with a black DKNY sleep mask, she was deeply snoring.

Soon, I fell into a dream-fueled sleep. It was filled not so much with story lines, but with vignettes and images. There were pastel hues, palm trees, shopping bags, and a pink-feather-tipped pen. And best of all? My vignettes featured all these goldenly attired randoms, smiling, laughing, hugging. Something told me that, like, this is my life. There were no clues as to when I would remember it.

When I woke, both De and Amber were gone, but I wasn't alone. Josh was slumped in a wing chair in the corner of the room. Wearing ripped jeans and a crinkled T-shirt, he looked massively haggard and fully stubble-charged. Hoisting myself up on my elbows, I tilted my head and regarded him. "You didn't sleep, did you?"

He nodded. "I was hoping Mel would call."

"Mel," I repeated. "You really think a lot of him, don't you?"

Josh rubbed his eyes and let out a long sigh. "We both do, Cher."

"I take it he hasn't called back yet."

Josh's eyes narrowed. "Not yet. He must be in transit. But that jerk who caused the accident called—about three times."

I was momentarily flummoxed. Then I remembered Lee, the brave, Baldwinian surfer who'd said how sorry he was. I sat up in the bed and folded my arms in front of my chest. "It wasn't Lee's fault this happened, Josh."

"Oh, really?" he sneered. "And I suppose you conveniently remember that part, do you?"

I swallowed. "No," I said quietly, "I don't remember exactly what happened, but—like, my instincts tell me it was a no-fault accident."

"A no-fault accident? Trust me on this, Cher. You do not surf. You would not risk getting a strand of your precious hair wet, or heaven forbid, your make-up smudged! If that smooth-talking Lothario hadn't lured you onto a surf board, none of this would have happened."

I began to giggle.

"You're finding this funny?" Josh was beyond annoyed.

"No. It's just that—I'm guessing brutal bickering isn't new to us?"

Josh tried unsuccessfully to conceal his grin. "New to us? Hardly. It basically defines our relationship."

"Thought so. So what did you tell Lee, anyway? Nothing encouraging, I assume?"

The grin dissipated and Josh got defensive. "Not to bother calling back."

I was about to go ballistic. Like, who was Josh to tell a hottie not to call me back? But then the absurdity of the whole situation hit me again. Like until I regained my memory, what good was a surf studmuffin anyway?

I sighed. "Look, Josh, why don't you get some breakfast while I wash up. You look like you could use some nutrition—not to mention a wardrobe transfusion."

Josh laughed. "Breakfast? It's four in the afternoon, Cher. Lunch maybe."

Just at that moment, the phone rang. Josh bolted out of his seat and grabbed it on one ring. A second later his face morphed into full animation, as he burbled, "He did? That's great! When? Okay . . . okay . . . all right. We'll wait for his call and then get ready."

He hung up, explaining, "That was Miss Geist. She said Mel just called. He'd been in transit to New York, and his plane was in a holding pattern for hours so he didn't get our message until a few minutes ago. He's on the phone with the doctors from Maui Memorial, and then he's calling us here. Then he's flying back to

LA and wants us to meet him there. But he wants to talk to you first. He'll call this room in a few minutes."

An icky feeling engulfed me. I suddenly realized that I wasn't ready to talk to this Mel that I'd heard so much about.

"Uh, Josh, I'm hitting the shower. When . . . Mel . . . calls, you talk to him, okay?"

Josh went all perplexed. "Why don't you want to talk to your father?"

Since I had no real answer for that, I didn't try. I jumped out of bed and ran into the bathroom and locked the door. I took, like, the longest shower in the history of Hawaii.

Later, I felt fully dejected as I packed to go home. De and Amber had returned, explaining that they'd spent the day on a hike up to one of Maui's foremost eco-sights, the Iao Needle. According to De, I was lucky to have slept through it. "It was cloudy and misty. The humidity seeped into our hair: frizz city. You would have been beyond bugged."

I ran my fingers through my long, silky, humidity-free locks. "Josh said something about my not wanting to get my hair wet, too, or my makeup trashed. I guess I must be thoroughly vigilant about my appearance?"

De and Amber exchanged perplexed looks. De spoke up. "We all are, Cher. Like you, we're committed to our personal best, leading the way for others. It's our small contribution to a woefully chaotic world."

I nodded. "Um, I'm also guessing that I don't normally leave projects unfulfilled, because I'm feeling bummed at bailing without seeing the completion of the documentary thing."

De waved my anxiety away as she helped me zipper the last of my Louis Vuitton suitcases. "Tscha! You'll totally see it completed. We'll finish it up and bring it back to Los Angeles."

Amber was all, "Besides, it's not as if you had a crucial part or anything. You were merely a writer. Totally dispensable, I assure you."

De rolled her eyes and was all, "Just get home and get back to yourself. I'm sure your father has, like, a platoon of specialists waiting at the gate. And besides, we'll all be back in three short days, and we'll call you ASAP."

"I'll call you, too—both of you. Do I, uh, have your numbers?"

De put her arm around me and whispered, "We're programmed into the speed dial of your cellular. I packed it in your slingback. Cher, I just know this nightmare will be over soon. It has to be. This is you! And besides, everyone—Murray, Sean, all our crowd—is fully pulling for you."

Call me mental, but for some reason? It didn't look like Amber was doing her share of that pulling thing. Whatever.

In our first-class seats on the plane ride home, I prodded Josh to open my personal file. For some reason, he wasn't sure what he should tell me. But by the time we landed in Los Angeles, I'd absorbed this much: I was Cher Horowitz, sixteen, and current circumstances aside, just as in my dream, my life was vigorously stellar.

I lived in a way decent Beverly Hills abode and had a rampant contingent of t.b.'s and admirers at Bronson Alcott High School. I had my own fully loqued-out Jeep, and, as suspected, the gift of garb: always ensembly correct and awesomely accessorized to the max. Although Josh delivered this last tidbit of info as the least important part—making some lame joke about me being the clotheshorse formerly known as Cher—I fully suspected it was higher on my priority chain than he had represented.

There was more good stuff, too. Although I lived in a one-parent household, I was the daughter of a fully prominent Beverly Hills attorney, Mel Horowitz, the sovereign of overprotective, whose joy it was to bestow upon me the lifestyle to which I'd become accustomed.

When he spoke of Mel, Josh went into full anxiety-rush. "Mel's berserk, Cher."

Without thinking, I rejoined, "Well, I just hope he's not pigging out on ice cream and cookies and other artery-choking, chemically enhanced foodstuffs."

Josh jumped up in his seat and hit his head on the flight attendant call button. "Cher, you remembered!"

"I did?"

"Mel calms his anxiety with food. It's one of the things you fight with him about constantly. It's how you take care of him . . ." Josh trailed off, realizing that

I'd gone clueless again. It was like, that thought suddenly popped into my head. But like a single sample Steve Madden platform, it was all alone. No matching thoughts accompanied it.

I had no idea why I knew anything about Mel's dietary habits.

Chapter 10

Mel Horowitz was impatiently pacing at the gate when we landed at LAX. I'd been hearing so much about him, a part of me clung to the hope that as soon as I saw him? Tscha! I'd remember everything.

Not even.

Mel—my father—turned out to be not merely overprotective, but overwrought, and tragically overweight. He did know how to dress, though. I saluted his monochromatic shirt and tie combination. Intuitively, I pegged it as Zegna. And his shoes practically bellowed Bally.

Tearfully, he embraced me. I wasn't sure how I'd react to being wrapped in the bear hug of a strange adult, but, hello, that same feeling of comforting familiarity washed over me as it had with Josh the other day. I sniffed his aura: Hugo Boss aftershave.

Disentangling me from his grasp, he gripped my shoulders and inspected me at arm's length. Hopefully, he was all, "You know me, Cher, right?"

I shook my head.

He tried again. "Okay, what about this shirt and tie? You bought them for me."

That part made sense, but I had no memory of buying them for him.

Or of him at all.

During the entire limo ride home, Mel anxiously barraged me with a thousand questions.

"Does anything hurt? Are you sure? It's okay, I'm your father, you can tell me. Is your vision blurry? Even a little? Do you remember anything?"

Finally Josh objected that he was, like, badgering the witness. Which is when Mel vented his frustrations on my faux stepbrother.

"Why was I not contacted immediately when this happened?" he demanded.

Josh swallowed. "We tried, Mel. You didn't answer your pager and, well, I took her to the hospital and she's basically fine—"

"Basically fine!" he thundered. "This is what you call basically fine? She doesn't know who she is, Josh. What's the matter with you? What kind of nincompoop did I raise?"

"You raised him?" I whispered almost inaudibly. "I thought we weren't related."

At the same time, they both shot at me:

"We're not!"

"You're not!"

And then they went back to their argument.

Josh, for the defense—of himself—was all, "We did what you would have done. The doctors all said the same thing: she's okay. She could regain her memory at any time. They even thought it was possible she'd regain it by the time she went home."

Mel growled, "Well, she didn't, did she? And as far as I can see, you haven't regained your sense of propriety. Why didn't you Medevac her home? How could you take her to some one-horse foreign hospital?"

"Foreign? Hawaii's not a foreign country, Mel, it's the U.S. Their medical facilities are the same as—"

"Don't give me that! It's not Cedars-Sinai, is it?"

I slunk back in my seat, closed my eyes, and tuned them out. This bickering thing seemed to be, like, genetic.

The next day was such the ologist-fest: neurologists, psychologists, ophthalmologists, endocrinologists, gastroenterologists. Mel had them, plus other random practitioners of cutting-edge medicine—internists, surgeons both orthopedic and plastic, nutritionists, and published psychiatrists—come to the house, insisting that I shouldn't be moved, and besides, "In my day, real doctors made house calls."

"They're the best money can buy," Mel kept assuring me and Josh.

One of the shrinks turned out to be Dr. Salk, Amber's father. He suggested adding an aromatherapist to the mix. An idea that sounded stellar to me, only Mel spiked it.

Then there was the woman I mistook for a physician. While waiting her turn to examine me, or so I thought, she'd made herself comfortable in the great room, feet up on the marble coffee table, fingers in the trail mix, engrossed in the drama on the big screen TV. But she turned out to be Lucy, our housekeeper.

"She works for us, Cher," Mel explained. "She can't help you get your memory back."

Like, duh, so far as I could tell? Neither could any of the other über-educated, degree-laden specialists. Not an ologist among them had added anything new or vital beyond "temporary amnesia." And addendum: for fear of being sued, no one would come forth to define "temporary." They all concurred that I should return to my normal habitat and eventually it would all come back to me, one memory at a time.

On the upside, however, Josh had nailed the living quarters description. Not only was the House of Horowitz furiously upper echelon, I totally applauded the decor in the room Mel said belonged to me. Whoever I was, I had a ferocious flair for interior decorating. The rich mix of Laura Ashley and Ralph Lauren wallpaper, sheets, and bedspread was genius. Nurturing and classic at the same time.

On my second day "home," I was admiring this very handiwork when Mel appeared in the doorway.

Carting a huge cardboard box, he looked beyond stressed. He had the same haggard vibe as Josh had worn in Hawaii.

"Can I come in, Cher?"

I shrugged and flopped on the bed. "It's your house."

Okay, so I totally regretted that the minute I said it.

The deep pools of sadness in Mel's eyes were beyond tragic.

"It's your house, too, Cher. In fact," he said, perching on the edge of the divan across from the bed, dropping the box on the floor, "in a way, it's more your house than mine. You're the one who really runs this place."

"I do?"

"Are you kidding? You organize everything, the staff, my social calendar, my wardrobe, all my meals—you even decide what videos we watch. We call you the CEO around here."

"I'm sure that competency becomes me, I just wish I could remember."

"Look, Cher, there's something I need to confess. This whole thing has been a nightmare. But what hurts most is that since you got off the plane, you haven't once called me Daddy."

My eyes downcast, I whispered, "Which is what I would normally call you."

"You do believe that I'm your father, don't you, Cher? Because if you don't"—he indicated the box at his feet—"I have all the paperwork to prove it. Beyond a shadow of a doubt. I even have your birth certificate. Come here and I'll show you."

"It's not that I don't believe you," I protested weakly, crossing the room and settling myself on the floor next to the box he'd brought. "I just—"

"Here," he interrupted, reaching into the cardboard box, "your birth certificate." He held up a gilt-framed official-looking document.

"You had it framed?"

"Of course. And here, look at these. Baby pictures,

growing up pictures . . ." He'd pulled a leather-bound album of photos from the box and started flipping through it.

"What else did you mount?" I asked, spying more framed ornaments.

He fished one out. "Here, your second-grade drawing of a Visa Gold card. It was your first attempt, successful I might add, at renegotiating your grade. Your teacher had given you a mere check and you wanted a check plus. So you told her that coloring outside the lines was the hallmark of a creative personality. You were right, and she bought it. See, there's your check plus."

Suddenly, I was overcome with a pressing urge to hug Mel. I threw my arms around him and buried my head in his wrinkled shirt as I murmured, "I believe you—I mean, of course I believe you, Daddy."

"I have another idea," he said as he unclasped me. "Tomorrow I've arranged for all our relatives—your grandparents, uncles, aunts, cousins, some ex-stepmothers—to come by and see you. Who knows? It's possible one of them will spark your memory."

He'd missed someone. I wondered if that was on purpose. Tentatively, I said, "Um, speaking of that. What about my real mother? Everyone's been telling me about myself, but no one's said much about her. Will she be making an appearance?"

Daddy's face fell. "Your mother died, Cher."

"Oh. I'm sorry, Mel—I mean, Daddy. I just assumed that, you know, like, it was a divorce thing. Was it . . . recent?"

"A long time ago, Cher, when you were a baby."

"So I guess I didn't know her very well?"

Daddy stood up abruptly and tapped my arm. "Come with me, Cher."

He led me down the staircase and pointed to the portrait of a bodacious Betty that hung at the base of the steps. Of course, I'd noticed it, along with the other ferocious artwork, when I arrived yesterday—also that it seemed a little crooked—but it didn't occur to me that I was related to it.

"This is your mother," Mel was explaining, "and in a funny way, you seem to have a relationship with her."

I peered at the portrait and tried to sort out my thoughts. He continued, "You talk to her, to the picture. Or, as you always say, 'Mom's got a non-speaking, yet featured performer, role in my life.' Does any of this make any sense to you, sweetheart?"

I sighed dejectedly. I was such the blank slate.

The next day Daddy catered a full-service fiesta under tents set up in the backyard. There, a platoon of relations paraded through for my inspection. Among them were a set and a half of ancestral grandparents, flown up from Florida. Then there was the stylish Grandma Ray, imported from her lush retirement condo in Laguna Beach, who tried to foist something called a kreplach on me. Next came a gamut of fractious, bejeweled stepmothers—including Gail, mom to Josh, who was also there—a phalanx of cousins, aunts, and uncles. I didn't recognize any of them, but hello, they so reminded me of De's beach house brood: dripping in chronic threads but lacking in anything resembling family harmony.

Tragically? After all the canapés had been devoured

and the last of the clan had swept through, I was no closer to remembering anything. But then, like, light-bulb: maybe that wasn't so bizarre after all.

"Daddy? Can I ask you something?" He, Josh, and I had finished overseeing the massive post-relative cleanup effort and had settled ourselves back in the house.

"Of course, Cher, anything."

"I totally give you snaps for organizing the *mishpucha* encounter. But, like, *should* I know them? Do I normally see them? On any regular basis?"

Daddy sank into a chair and rubbed his stubbled cheeks. "Like all families, we see each other at weddings, bar mitzvahs, that sort of thing."

"In other words, Cher," Josh broke in, "that would be a no. Aside from your grandparents, you've barely met any of those people before. I never understood how any of them could make you remember anything."

Daddy exploded and turned his rage on Josh. "Did you have a better idea, counselor? All these cockamamie specialists couldn't tell us a blessed thing! Well, I just can't stand by and see her struggling like this. She deserves to have her life back! I have to do something!"

I put my arm around Daddy and went for comforting. "We're both with you. And even though I may not remember you, I know this much: you'd want us all to think positively. Or we'll just have to indict my memory for gross abandonment. How's that?"

There were tears in Daddy's eyes when he said, "Just look at you, Cher. Worried about me when you're the one with this . . . condition. But that's you—always trying to make things better for other people."

I was giving myself snaps for that magnanimous trait, when Josh broke in.

"Look, Mel, you've done everything. You brought in the best modern medicine has to offer. And every specialist has given you the same advice, yet you refuse to act on it. Haven't they all said that Cher's best chance of getting her memory back is by being in her normal environment? Mel, you've got to send her back to school, to her friends, to her natural habitat, and—I can't believe I'm saying this—send Cher back to the mall!"

Chapter 11

Daddy knew a sound argument when he heard one. Reluctantly, he agreed that the next day I could go back to school. Serendipitously, it was the day my peer group would be back from Hawaii. I decided to try that speed-dial thing to see if De was home.

She answered on, like, a half ring. "Cher! I just walked in and I was about to call you. I'm coming over!"

When she did, a while later, she bounced up the stairs to my room. Her face registered optimism, but I knew it was faux. I fully sensed her grave disappointment at my continued state of memory-deficiency.

Gently, she was all, "So, how are you, girlfriend?"

I shrugged, while admiring her Missoni purple pants and tunic ensemble. It viciously matched the mini shopping bag she was carrying.

"As well as can be expected, I guess. But let's don't dwell. It's getting majorly boring. Tell me about the second half of the Hawaiian experience."

De proceeded to describe some grievous predawn voyage the group had been forced to take to Haleakala, the world's largest dormant volcano, where it was so cold that Amber's hair froze in place.

Picturing that, I had to laugh.

"I hope Murray got it on tape. Speaking of which, did you finish the documentary?"

De was all, "I think so. I mean, Murray shot more footage, but we won't really know what we got until it's all edited." She paused. "Umm, Cher, there is something else I have to tell you."

She lowered her voice to just above a whisper, as if hidden mikes could pick up what she was about to say.

"Last night in Hawaii, the hotel hosted some random luau fiesta. We got these faux official certificates from Chad—he was the leader of the Sierra Club eco-journey—okay, you probably don't remember. Anyway it proves that we actually completed the expedition. I brought yours." De fished out my eco-diploma from the shopping bag.

Another milestone for Daddy to frame, I thought.

De continued, "But the thing is, Cher, *he* came looking for you."

"Who did? This Chad person?"

"As if! No, Chad had the hots for Miss Geist."

I must have gone massively flummoxed because De was all, "Forget that. We've moved on. Anyway, the thing is, your prince of tides was there, hoping to see you. Lee went way tragic when I told him you'd gone home. He's really sprung on you."

"Sprung on me? Or not. Maybe Lee just feels responsible. That's pretty much the feeling I got from him when he epilogued at your beach house."

"Whatever. He was seriously bummed that you weren't there—and of course at your continued state of detail-impairment. Anyway, he gave me something for you."

De proffered the mini shopping bag at me.

I separated the tissue paper and extracted its contents. Lee had sent a furiously foliage-charged garland. It came with a note he'd quickly scribbled on hotel stationery when De told him I'd left already.

> Aloha, Cher. I don't know if I'll ever see you again, but I wanted to leave you with this Hawaiian lei. These tiny blooms, shells, and ferns were sewn together by hand—it's as unique as you are. Although it may only last a few hours, the memory lasts forever. As mine will of you, Cher.

I inhaled the fragrant garland. What I would have given for any memory, even a fragment.

I looked up. De was eyeballing me hopefully.

"And another one surfs into the sunset?" she guessed.

"Another one? De, can I ask you something? I mean, I've had, like, other boyfriends, right?"

"Tscha, Cher! A battery of Baldwins. You're the major studmuffin magnet of Bronson Alcott and all of 90210-land," she assured me.

A swatch of a thought floated by. "I'm not—okay, I know this must sound totally lame—but I'm not seeing anyone named Calvin, am I? Or Ralph?"

De laughed. "Only on your labels, girlfriend, the best place to be seeing them!"

Just then De's beeper went off.

"Murray?" I guessed.

"No, my mother. Attila-the-stalker summons. I've gotta bail, Cher. See you tomorrow at school." De and I hugged and she left.

I devoted my evening hours to trying to figure out what I would normally wear on a school day. There was an alarming plethora of possibilities in my remote-controlled closet. It seemed crucial that I not make a grievous ensemble mistake. And segue: being stylistically insecure did so not feel appropriate.

I was holding up a Max Mara shift and coat ensemble while modeling a nubby Chanel suit when I heard the doorbell ring. A minute later I heard Daddy call, "Cher, it's your friend Amber. You want to come down?"

Before I could answer, she started up the stairs, "No problema, Mr. Horowitz. Cher should so not tax herself at my expense. I'll brave the steps."

Like De, Amber hadn't arrived empty-handed. Only her shopping bag was way huger than the one De had brought. It was logo-ed, something-Mart.

Amber didn't waste time with preliminaries but launched into the reason for her drive-by.

"As soon as I got home, I heard the news: my daddy told your daddy that the best treatment for you is going back to school. Therefore, I, Amber Salk, have appointed myself enabler-in-chief. I'm going to help ease you back into society. As my first good deed, I've brought you the choice ensemble in which to make your debut at Bronson Alcott tomorrow."

Prologue accomplished, Amber extracted a three-piece aggregate that brought the word *garish* to my lips: a fuzzy black mohair bustier, a silver shag bolero jacket—I flashed on '70s-style carpeting—and black vinyl hip-huggers.

For some reason, the name Pamela Lee popped into my mind.

I laid the hideous ensemble out on the bed and studied it from all angles.

"Uh, snaps for the thought, Amber, but are you sure this is my style?"

Amber rolled her heavily made-up eyes. "Earth to Cher: am I not your premium t.b.? Would I not know your style? This is très au courant. And you, above all else, are obsessed with being on the cutting edge of the fashion scene."

While I could accept some of that, I couldn't shake the feeling that *no*, this is not an outfit I would paint myself into. Gingerly, I went, "I've been scanning my closet, and of all the bodacious outfits hanging there? Like, nothing remotely resembles this."

"Excuse me, Cher, but like, duh! When is the last time you upgraded your wardrobe? Do you even know? Of course not! Well, it just so happens, I do, and hello, every item in your closet screams last semester. On your first day back at school, you do want something circa this week, n'est-ce pas?"

Totally n'est-ce pas. But still, I had doubts about

the discount-feel feather-fest she was foisting on me. My disbelief was clearly showing—not unlike, I suddenly noticed, Amber's visible panty line.

"Sit down, Cher," she urged, leading me over to the divan. "I didn't want to tell you this, especially in front of Dionne. But the truth is, at school? I am the most revered Betty to grace the corridors. Everyone bows to my expertise in all things sartorial, academic, social—well, what can I say? Everything. And you, Cher Horowitz, you're the one who most looks up to me."

"I look up to you, Amber?"

"You worship me, Cher."

Amber flashed an ingratiating dental display and began to flounce out of my room. "Trust me, Cher. Wear the outfit I bought for you. Everyone will think this amnesia thing was just a ploy, that you've really been to the Paris and Milan fashion shows."

Trust her? As I dubiously fingered the squeaky vinyl pants she'd left, something told me this entire scenario—me worshipping her—was brutally faux. But then again, hadn't De said that Amber was a t.b.? I considered calling De, but who was I to doubt Amber's word?

I couldn't even answer the first part of that sentence.

When I came down for breakfast in the morning, Daddy was in the middle of his poached eggs. His eyebrows shot up and his fork crashed down when he saw me.

"I don't normally dress like this, do I?" I asked tentatively.

He wiped his mouth with a linen napkin. "Well, Cher, that's hard to say. You're always original and stylish. But whether what you're wearing is in style or not? I'm not the right one to ask."

Like, understatement. What Daddy didn't know, the entire student body of Bronson Alcott seemed to. From the moment I alighted from the limo Daddy insisted on sending me to school in, I was totally the object of harsh ridicule, such the laughingstock. In spite of my humiliation, I did realize that it wasn't me they were going all hyena at, but my heinous outfit. Jaws dropped, fingers pointed, some of my peers—who'd been clued in to my condition via the always accurate grapevine—actually gripped their stomachs, reduced to makeup-smudging hysterics.

Holding my head high, I bravely crossed a verdantly lush outdoor area and headed into the main school building. I couldn't help overhearing dollops of derisive comments:

"I thought they said she had amnesia, not a complete style meltdown."

"Did, like, Pamela Lee invade her body?"

"Yo, Cher, shopping with Dennis Rodman?"

In spite of the stinging critical barbs, I continued on. A famous poem came to me: there are no hideous outfits, only hideous people making fun of them. Or something.

I made my way to the administration office for a map of the school and a copy of my schedule, so I'd know where I was going—and why. As my guidance counselor explained, we wouldn't know how much of the work I'd remember, if any. "But we're committed to helping you catch up, Cher, so don't worry about lapses in your work," Vice Principal Gardner assured me. By the way she eyeballed my outfit, I could tell even she was worried about my apparent lapse in good taste.

In homeroom I caught up with De. Her reaction upon catching sight of me was to let out a bloodcurdling scream.

Like, you could barely hear Miss Geist go, "You may be excused, Dionne, and uh, you, too, Cher, dear."

"Where are we going?" I asked Dionne as she jumped behind the wheel of her Jaguar, and we screeched out of the school driveway.

De was ranting about Amber. "I should have known she'd pull something like this. Trying to make you over into a cartoon copy of her! I blame myself for leaving you alone with her! But, Cher, how could you let Amber do this to you?"

"A part of me knew it was faux, but on what grounds could I doubt her? You're the one who said Amber was a t.b.—true blue?"

De barely slowed down as she careened around the corner, "Maybe—*maybe*—her misguided intentions were worthy, but true green is more like it when it comes to Ambu-lame. Like, how many ways can you spell envy?"

"De, do we routinely play practical jokes on her? I mean, is this payback?"

Slyly De was all, "Payback? Not even. She's just delirious, Cher. She thinks by demoting you on the popularity meter, she moves up."

I ventured, "So I don't like . . . worship her?"

De slammed on the brakes. Her jaw fell as she turned to me, horrified. "As if! Hello, the other way around. Everyone at Bronson Alcott worships you. You are, literally, the Polaroid of perfection."

Then she hit the accelerator again and was all, "We are going to rectify this catastrophe right now. We will show them that Cher Horowitz may be momentarily detail-deficient, but she has not lost her aptitude for haute couture. We are going shopping, girlfriend."

On the way to the mall, De explained that the feeling we always get from a major shopping spree is the best antidote to practically everything.

And as it turned out? De totally rocked. As we trolled the Beverly Center, filling shopping bag upon shopping bag with classic ensembles, shoes, boots, and accessories, I felt warm, fuzzy, and fulfilled all over. My humiliation had completely vanished.

Even better, De vigorously applauded my choices. "Yes! This is what you would totally choose. This is so you!"

As we passed Contempo Casuals, I pointed out a familiar-looking frock and leggings ensemble. "Did I once have something like that?"

De tilted her head and regarded it. "You're close. Amber did, only it was all leopard print and tiger leggings. But that's a majorly positive sign, girlfriend. Real stuff is starting to come back to you!"

Tragically, only ten minutes later, De had to reverse herself when I had a flash, and asked, "De, did I once do something fully bizarre? Like threaten to blow up an apartment complex?"

Sadly, De said, "No, Cher, that was crazy Kimberly on *Melrose Place.*"

I tried again. "But I used to have a puppy, didn't I?"

De's eyes lit up, then quickly clouded over. "Unless you come up with name, breed, and circumstance, I'll have to brand that as a guess, Cher."

Hello, it was a good try.

All throughout our spree, De's cellular kept ringing. Mostly it was Murray.

After the fourth time, she barked into it, "Obsession is a brand name, Murray, not an acceptable brand of behavior."

When she pressed End, I ventured, "You and Murray, have you always been so Velcroed?"

De snorted. "Not even. We do that peaks and valleys thing constantly. But whenever we're frosted, you're always on board to facilitate the patch up. You're the problem solver of our entire posse."

For some reason a phrase came to me: "The acclaimed untier of thorny knots?"

De frowned. "I don't know that *I've* ever put it that way, but totally."

Then De went on to explain that if it weren't for me, she'd never have gotten to her father's ex-wife's beach house in Hawaii. "The whole thing—to combine our endangered species lesson with a field trip to Hawaii—was fully your design concept and execution."

I eyed her pensively. "How did it all work out? I mean, doy, obvious complications aside."

De exhaled dramatically. "On the one hand, it was golden! I got to see my father and all these fabulons

I'm quasi-related to. I never would have experienced that otherwise."

"But on the other hand?" I inquired.

De explained, "My mother, who was brutally versus my connecting with that side of the family, found out about our beach house sidebar. She went nuclear."

"Did she ground you or something?"

"As if! We don't do grounding, Cher. We've all moved beyond pubescent penalization. But grievously, she's insistent on having me around. Like, aside from school, twenty-four seven. I can deal with it, but with this Ambu-debacle, I'm suddenly apprehensive about not being able to give you my undivided attention."

De's cellular rang.

"Or Murray, either?" I finished for her.

De was conversing with her boo when she said something about being "on the money."

It struck a chord. I dropped my shopping bags, waved my arms around, and shouted, "Show me the money!"

De nearly dropped her cell.

I sang out, "De! I remember! Doesn't Murray always say, 'Show me the money!' "

De looked stricken. Oops, my wrong.

I tried again. "Sean! It's Sean who always says that!"

"No, Cher, no one says that in real life. It's from a movie. Tom Cruise and Cuba Gooding Jr. say it."

De went back to Murray. "No, boo, she didn't actually remember anything useful. Her recall is totally partial. She's having random flashbacks, limited accessory memory mixed with TV show and movie dialogue."

As I watched De converse cellularly with Murray, I wondered if there was a memory redial on the phone.

Chapter 12

Thanks to De, I came to school the next day appropriately attired in an iridescent shantung shirt jacket over a sleeveless Prada T-shirt. I was greeted by a massive chorus of relieved sighs from my followers. I got props and good wishes from Murray and Sean, plus randoms who ID'ed themselves as Janet, Annabelle, Summer, Baez, Ringo, and Brian. Then there was the hottie-esque Jesse, who seemed more than generically interested.

I made it through first and second period—Mr. Hall's lit class and Ms. Lautz's math class—without trauma. Okay, so, like, I didn't exactly remember any of the lessons, but I could decipher my notes and had no trouble following along. My teachers, especially Mr. Hall, who still walked with a cane because of his lava-snafu, were frantically simpatico.

When I stumbled on Amber in third period, she fell

all over herself apologizing for the ensemble fiasco. "I totally assure you, Cher, it was done with the foremost of intentions. But excuse me, sometimes you're the windshield, sometimes you're the bug. Even you can't help being the occasional fashion victim."

The words "And who would know better than you" sprang to my lips, but I squashed them. What, after all, did I really know?

Later, during eighth-period science, Amber buzzed me on the cellular. "I just called to remind you about the basketball playoffs."

"And the significance in my life would be . . . ?"

"Duh, Cher, you're on the girls basketball team. Star player. Don't worry, I had your uniform dry-cleaned and delivered to your locker. Just show up at the gym next period and suit up. Oh, and don't be surprised if Coach Diemer—that's our gym teacher—acts surprised to see you. She's cutting you massive slack since your unfortunate detail-deficiency debacle. But I know you're up for this, right?"

"I don't remember playing basketball—" I started.

"Excuse me, Cher," Amber interjected. "Remind me again exactly what it is you *do* remember? Besides, it's like driving a Jeep. It will totally come back to you! The team needs you. And the Cher *I* know would never let her teammates flounder."

I was flummoxed. If yesterday's couture catastrophe *had* been a cruel joke, I wouldn't put it past Amber to play another trick on me. I had my finger on the speed dial to ask De, but she'd exited early to attend a press conference for Julia Roberts with her mother. After what De had said about her mother's nuclear reactor, I wasn't sure she was allowed to accept calls from friends, especially the one who'd thought up the beach house sidebar.

I tried Murray, but he didn't pick up. I remembered De saying something about him being in a sound-proof editing room getting our documentary ready. I was about to call Daddy for confirmation of this basketball thing when I suddenly had a flash of memory: it was me, in a stellar basketball uniform. I was leaping three feet off the ground, the ball had just left my extended arms to arch gracefully skyward. Okay, so that could have been something I saw on TV, but then again, it could have been one of those real-life snippets I was having. If it was, the team needed me.

As I headed toward the school lockers, I frantically scanned the hallway for someone I trusted. I caught a glimpse of Sean, who had his arm around Summer and was rushing in the other direction. "Sean! Summer!" I yelled out. "Am I on the basketball team?"

I'm not sure if they heard me, because Summer just waved and Sean was all, "Go team, go!"

I took that as a potential yes and changed into the uniform Amber had left in my locker. It was in school colors: black and white. Stitched across the top was the team's name: Alcott Acrylics. I laced up a pair of LA Gears that were also in the locker and twirled in front of the full-length mirror. I did look stellar. Like, ergo, I probably was on the team.

Not even.

Two minutes later, when I hit the gym floor, I was greeted by the sight of several long-legged, limber classmates expertly bouncing the ball, passing it around, and occasionally arching it upward. Bravely, I insinuated myself in the throes of the action, snatching the stitched orange orb from under a towering teammate and attempting contact with that net-fringed ringy thingy attached to the backboard.

Just as it had in my memory, my shot arched gracefully in the air, when a piercing whistle jarringly brought all motion to a screeching halt.

The authority figure I surmised to be Coach Diemer was in my face, bellowing, "Horowitz! What do you think you're doing here? Get out of the way!"

I spun around. Everyone was glaring down at me. The truth sank in as my faux jump shot had not. "I'm . . . not . . . on the basketball team?" I guessed.

Diemer barked, "Why would you think you were? Your athletic aptitude is limited to new and improved excuses to cut PE, not free throws. I thought you had amnesia, not delusions of sports grandeur. Move it, Horowitz. We have playoffs to win."

Oops, my gullible. I stalked out of the gym and dove for my cellular. I speed dialed the coif-challenged trickster and fully vented my wrath.

Amber's faux-remorseful response? "Did I say basket*ball* team? I meant basket-*weaving* team. Oops. Color me chagrined."

Later De checked in. When I described my latest bout with Ambu-miliation, it was, like, color her beyond ballistic. My main big seethed, "She was probably paying you back for leaving her out of the Hawaii loop in its initial planning stages, but she has gone overboard this time. I will so get back at her for this. I'm calling Murray and Sean."

"The Big Kahunas of revenge?" I guessed.

"Cher! You remembered . . ." she started to say, but trailed off, realizing that a swatch of phrase does not a full bedspread of memory make.

I'd been back at school for two days. After each, I'd come home to the expectant gaze of my father.

Hopefully, he'd be all, "Anything today, Cher?"

Then I'd tell him what partial bits of memory I'd recouped. Daddy made a valiant stab at hiding his disappointment, but I knew he was totally wiggin'. That's why I raided the kitchen daily. If he was coping with his anxieties by ingesting faux, artery-clogging foodstuffs, it was my job to intervene. At least, I thought it was my job.

I was scanning the various nooks and kitchen crannies the afternoon of my basketball boo-boo when I came across a cabinet riddled with recipe-obsessed books like *Butter Busters: The Cookbook*, *Lean Bodies Cookbook*, and *Controlling Your Fat Tooth*.

Thought! Maybe this is how I help Daddy overcome his food-anxiety affliction. Using these recipes, I probably prepare furiously healthy meals. Flipping through the pages, I came to an intriguing possibility called tofu torte. While I wasn't exactly sure what that was, I could read and follow directions. I decided to see how doable it was.

Tragically, finding utensils in this kitchen that involved actual cooking was beyond impossible. Even looking for them felt massively weird. Still, I gathered a bunch of potential cooking tools and laid them out on the counter. I gripped one and tried it on for size. I was just checking my reflection in the microwave, when Josh sauntered in.

His face registered a ten on the shock meter. "What are you doing, Cher?"

Tentatively, I went, "Preparing Daddy a healthy meal? I mean, I thought I'd whip something up."

Carefully, Josh instructed, "Okay, Cher, put the spatula down before somebody gets hurt. You don't whip things up—unless it's dinner reservations."

Okay, so Josh was probably dissing me, but I couldn't help my instinctive reaction. A massive sigh of relief escaped my lips.

"So you're saying I'm more of an enabler than an actual . . . cook."

Josh folded his arms in front of his chest and eyeballed me. "Precisely. Look, Cher. Mel's got a dinner meeting to go to tonight. Why don't you and I go grab a bite at someplace a little more familiar to you than the kitchen?"

I grinned. "You're on, Josh. Just let me run upstairs and change. I mean, that's what I would normally do, isn't it?"

"As you would say, Cher: totally."

A half hour later, Josh and I had settled into a booth at ObaChine, a fully chronic restaurant featuring Pacific Rim cuisine. From the line of black Range Rovers at the valet parking station to the actress-model types air-kissing each other to the haute retro decor—worn brick, handmade tiles, and painted metal banisters—I knew I was where I belonged.

Like the opposite feeling from being in the kitchen.

A lock of Josh's wavy hair fell into his eyes as he scanned the menu. The sudden urge to reach across the table and brush it aside seized me, but I resisted. Instead I mumbled, "Do you eat here often?"

Josh looked up, his azure eyes twinkling. "Are you kidding? It's a little high on the trend-o-meter, not to mention overpriced, for me. I just thought—well, it seemed like the kind of place you'd go to, though of course I couldn't ask you. So, I took a shot. Along with Mel's credit card." He winked.

I felt a stab of affection for Josh. "This is so proper—I mean, trying to take me someplace indigenous."

Grievously, Josh's personal sense of belonging in this restaurant was nil. He could not figure out what to order. Like he totally seemed unfamiliar with the concept that Asian rice is the pasta of the nineties. Hello, even amnesiac-me Cher sussed that out after but one menu glance.

Josh rolled his eyes as I ordered for both of us: spring rolls stuffed with gobo root, eel, and spicy sprouts, and Dungeness shumei, sprinkled with lemongrass, Thai fish sauce, and ponzu.

Clearly, I'd made competent choices. Josh scarfed the appetizers down contentedly. But when he refused to even taste another delicacy I'd ordered for our main, I had to force his horizons open. I made him close his eyes as I fed sesame-crusted oysters to him. Not knowing what he was eating had the anticipated positive effect: he fully enjoyed it.

Bizarrely, not knowing who I was had no effect on

me that night. Josh and I fully bonded, as he filled me in on his background, his lackluster love life—duh, I had to know about that—and his hopes of becoming a lawyer like Daddy one day.

And like, before I knew it? Dinner flew by.

When we got home, I heard myself saying, "Thanks, I had a chronic time. You almost made me forget—hello, bad choice of words!—well, anyway, about the whole amnesia thing."

Josh blushed furiously. "That's okay, Cher. No biggie. We all—Mel and I and everyone—we just want you to get your memory back. I'm, uh, heading to the dorm at UCLA—where I go to—well, you know. Anyway, see you tomorrow."

After tackling my homework, I combed through the box of framed photo memorabilia that Daddy had left on the floor of my room. Truth? I wasn't so much trying to find myself as looking for absolute proof that Josh and I were not biologically related.

Sans memory, all I had to trust were my own feelings. And right now? I was feeling furiously fluttery about Josh.

My third day back at school, Miss Geist announced during homeroom that our class would be debuting the documentary we made on Hawaii's endangered species. The entire school had been invited to the presentation.

De leaned over. "I'm getting good vibes, Cher. I fully believe seeing the documentary will spark your memory. Or at least give you some satisfaction," she said with a wink.

A special auditorium session had been arranged for the presentation. I took my seat up on the stage with my class and watched the auditorium fill up with Bronson Alcottians of all ages, stripes, and demeanors.

Miss Geist and Mr. Hall were like the MCs, explaining to the student body what they were about to experience. Then the lights dimmed and the music started. De whispered it was the theme song from when the Brady Bunch went to Hawaii.

The first scene was of our class getting on the plane. It was accompanied by narrator Amber's voiceover, dramatically describing her profound grief at the specter of being separated from her Dandie Dinmont puppy for a week.

Then came our class landing in Hawaii. Amber was all, "Here we are being greeted by the Hawaiian welcome wagon, giving us all authentic leis. Which, excuse me, were brutally *un*." When she said that, I had a flash of Amber dissing the lei she'd been given.

The next few scenes followed us as we frolicked at the hotel, sunbathed, got pedicures, and partied at Planet Hollywood, Maui. For me, it was all that wish-you-were-here thing, except, postscript, I had been. And my wardrobe selection for the jaunt had been golden.

Finally, the screen went to vividly shot scenes of humpback whales, fluking, breaching, and being such the innocents, unaware of the grave threat from polluters and hunters. I couldn't believe what I heard next.

On film Amber was all, "Okay, so these are the humpbacks. I would give you more information about them, but just around this time, our writer—and I am referring to Cher Horowitz—conveniently went into full memory block. She didn't provide the lines, and excuse me, ad libbing is so not in my contract."

I leaped up from my seat, about to claw Amber, but De grabbed my elbow and pulled me back down. "Shhh." She put her finger to her expertly lip-lined mouth. "Patience. Amber is about to get hers."

The next scene fully atoned for Amber's info-lapse. The screen was filled with the image of a blubbery baby monk seal on the shoreline, twisting and turning, coating itself with sand. The entire audience let out a collective "Aaaww." I flashed on a potential memory: the end of a *Full House* episode when that twin is hugging the father. It had the same "Aaaww" quality.

Then, a voiceover came on, but instead of Amber's haughty, it had the deep timbre of Lee, my surfer studmuffin, emotionally describing the history and plight of monk seals and green sea turtles. My heart swelled with pride. I fully deduced that this scene—the most crucial so far—had been my contribution. De's little squeeze of my shoulder pad was confirmation.

The rest of the documentary showcased Hawaiian flora, fauna, and more frolicking whales. Jesse made sure everyone knew that the soundtrack was by the Smashing Pumpkins.

Suddenly, in a total piece of special editing effects,

the onscreen mammals morphed into the faces of Murray and Sean! A collective gasp rose from the audience as De's main and his main accessory, draped in baggy draggies and riotously colored Hawaiian shirts, seamlessly slid into hip-hop mode, dancing and rapping. They were all:

"So now y'all have seen the whalies and the sealies
The humpbacks, the monk-backs, all nature's creatures got back!
The sand, the sun, the sea and yo!
The turtles be so fertile, but without help they could go! Oh, no!
They're threatened, they're threatened, dissed by breeders of deceit and greed!
They're callin', they're callin', out to *you* in their need!
But we got the solution to the whack pollution
Adopt a whale! Save the seals! Send a ducat for the tortoise! Write a check for a porpoise!"

To a chorus of "You go! You go! You go!" the audience erupted in thunderous applause and standing ovations. Many of our peer group fully reached for their credit cards and cellulars to make sizable donations as the names and addresses of various endangered species organizations, including the Sierra Club, appeared on the screen.

This was so stellar! Our documentary had reached its target audience, and the whole school was committing to saving the endangered mammals.

But Murray and Sean weren't done. Still on screen, they'd filmed themselves going, "And now, we'd like to introduce the band, heh, heh! That is, the creative geniuses behind the documentary you've just seen. Let's roll the credits!

"Give it up for our executive producers," Murray's voiceover urged, as the screen flashed on Miss Geist and Mr. Hall, holding hands by the pool and sneaking a smooch. The audience clapped and got queasy at the same time.

Then each of our stars got his or her deserved props via scenes of each in Hawaii: Summer, Janet, Ringo, Baez, Brian, and Annabelle. De and I had been caught on chaise longues in our most bodacious bathing suits. Jesse, headphone-obsessed, waved to the camera; Sean waved his guidebook; and Murray had filmed himself taking a deep bow.

Suddenly the music stopped and Murray's voice came on again. "Check it. I saved the brightest star of our documentary for last. Give it up for our narrator, Amber 'The Voice of Endangered America' Salk!"

As the live Amber started to get up to take a bow, the screen suddenly offered up a massive montage of caught-on-tape sleep 'n' snore moments—Amber snoring by the pool; masked Amber snoring in our hotel room; ensembly impaired Amber snoring at the surfer's cabin; Amber snoring contentedly on the deck of De's family beach house; and finally, coiffure-challenged Amber, her frozen flaming locks sticking out at odd angles, against the backdrop of the Haleakala volcano.

The entire auditorium erupted in hysterics. De, Murray, Sean, and I bounced up from our stage seats and furiously high-fived as Amber, her coloration as crimson as her hair, experienced up close and personal the feeling of being such the cheese.

Chapter 13

I'd hoped that seeing myself on tape in the documentary might nudge my still-comatose memory, but tragically, not even. Worse, as I found out the next day, color-her-chastised Amber was no mere soloist in the let's-pull-the-wool-over-Cher's-eyes game. She had an accomplice.

Just before lunch break, I was perched on a marble bench, waiting for De in that area called the Quad, when Jesse smarmily slid next to me and casually threw an arm around my shoulders. I shrugged him off.

Undissuaded, he was all, "Hey, Cher, babe. Deeply felt condolences on your loss."

"My loss?"

"On the brain-drain thing. But have no fear, your man is here to guide you through your darkest hour.

In fact, I brought you something to jolt your memory."

I shot Jesse a suspicious look, as he rifled through his Vuitton attaché case and extracted a Discman. He attempted to foist earphones on me, which I attempted to rebuff.

Jesse protested, "Babe, these are the unreleased tracks of Squirrel Nut Zippers, your favorite band. You've been begging me for this, and do I not always come through for you?"

Cautiously, I slipped the earphones on, only to be aurally assaulted by a sound not unlike chalk screeching on a blackboard.

I ripped the headphones off and shoved them at Jesse. "You allege that I'm actually into this band?"

Jesse leaned in close and slipped his arm around my waist. "Well, I think I should know, Cher. After all, you and I . . ." He trailed off.

"Excuse me? You and I *what,* Jesse?"

"Well, we're a thing." Jesse winked knowingly.

"A thing? You *mean,* we have a relationship?"

"A hot one, Cher. But we're keeping it on the down-low. Not even your best friends know about us," he whispered, nuzzling my earlobe.

Okay, so beyond instinct, I couldn't come up with a concrete reason to disbelieve Jesse. If De didn't know about it, how could she warn me? And tragically, no one besides that surfer dude Lee had come forward to claim me as a significant other. But, hello, if I couldn't trust my instincts, what could I trust? Which is why, when Jesse tried to kiss me, I pulled away.

He didn't push it. "It's okay if you're not ready yet.

I can wait." As he got up to leave, he was all, "Later, babe."

I watched Jesse strut away to join a group of similarly draped Baldwins, all hanging out under a nearby shade-bearing fruit tree.

Just then Dionne came rushing over and plopped down next to me on the bench. "Sorry I'm tardy, Cher. My mother's, like, cellularly stalking me." Then, motioning toward Jesse, she went suspicious, "I saw him sitting with you. What did he want?"

"Uh, to remind me about our passionate love affair?"

De snorted derisively and leaned forward on the bench to eyeball Jesse.

"What are you looking for?"

Indicating Jesse, she deadpanned, "Just checking to see if his pants are on fire."

De and I giggled and high-fived. Then she explained, "Jesse has been trying to get with you since sixth grade, Cher. You can't stand him."

"I hear you, De, but why not? I mean, he seems kind of like a good catch. He's brutally Baldwin, clearly a class leader, musically connected, and—"

"And? And? Cher! Jesse thinks self-gratification is a group activity. You wouldn't give him the time of day if . . ."

A feeling of total ick washed over me, as I finished Dionne's thought: "If I knew who I was, right? Only I don't, so I'm susceptible to deception. To believing what any random tells me. How can I even know that you're telling me the truth?"

De said nothing, but the look on her face said it all.

I felt a stab of remorse. "I'm—I'm sorry, Dionne. I

didn't mean to doubt you. I'm totally trying to stay above the waves about this, but sometimes it's all just so confusing."

De gave me a t.b. hug. "Girlfriend, I so feel your pain. Somehow, we *will* get you out of this memory morass."

I didn't doubt De's best-of-intentions, but if an armada of A-list MDs were solution-challenged, what could a mere t.b. do?

As if De could read my mind, she bolted frantically vertical and was all, "Look, Cher. Under normal circumstances, you're our leader with the plan. But now it's my turn. I pledge to come up with something that will help. Starting with, from now on you cannot be left unguarded. We will not run the risk of another random wannabe taking advantage of your memory-deficiency. I'm putting you on round-the-clock surveillance, as of now."

De whipped her cellular out of her Fendi bag and began rolling calls, setting up a schedule with Murray, Sean, Janet, Ringo, and other trusted friends.

When I applauded her positive, solution-oriented approach, De shot me an endearing, yet mournful, look. "I learned from the best, Cher. You."

I guess Murray must have learned from the best, too, because it was he who came up another memory-restorative plan.

When De called me later to describe it, she was all, "It's a Cher memory-palooza, an intervention to help you remember. It's going to be intense."

It was. The next day at lunch period, all my significant Bronson Alcott others, t.b.'s, crew members, and assorted teachers, gathered in the food court of the Quad. Over Spago-catered pizza, they unselfishly participated in the Cher memory-palooza.

De began the proceedings, for which she'd totally written a speech.

"Like any classic designer ensemble, the most rampantly correct pieces must come together to form the whole. That includes accessories. We are here today to accessorize Cher's memory. Each of us will contribute one swatch. And—"

De shot Amber and Jesse the evil—though expertly made-up—eye. "If anyone dares to try to trick her with faux information, he or she will be tossed from t.b.-hood, cut from the crew, doomed to suffer through high school alone, a freak, a loser, a wimp, a terminal outsider. And I don't think anyone here is willing to risk that."

Jesse, steeped in a pile of CDs, offered up his memory first.

"Music is the universal language, is it not? So, like, maybe a lyric, a riff, a CD cover of Cher's favorite groups will take her to some subliminal place and unlock her memory."

"Not Squirrel Nut Zippers," I warned, shaking a julietted finger at Jesse.

"Uh, no," he admitted. "You were never into them. But here, listen to this."

On a portable CD player, Jesse proceeded to play some nasty revenge-rock tune warbled by a jilted Betty. Not only didn't it unlock anything, I couldn't relate to it, since I didn't think I'd ever been jilted. Still, Jesse had sworn to be truthful, so this had to be one of my favorite singers.

"She's really angry, way harsh," I reacted. "I relate to that?"

De explained, "As if! But you do appreciate how reality-centric Alanis is."

I pondered that as I eyeballed a CD by the affably named Hootie & the Blowfish. "Which one is Hootie?" I asked.

Sadly Murray answered, "There is no Hootie, Cher."

"I used to know that, right?"

Jesse added, "Babe, you could also name each Blowfish."

Then it was De's turn. "Okay, Cher. The other day you asked me if you had a puppy. Well, you once did. You totally rescued one from a shelter."

An ember of memory glowed. "This puppy, was his name . . . AntonioLeo?"

De face lit up. "Close! It was BradKeanu! Cher, that's great!"

I was perplexed. "Where is BradKeanu? And why am I also thinking . . . something like muffs? Was he a mutt?"

De exploded with joy. "You're getting it! You're getting it! This is working! BradKeanu was a little too destructive to keep, but you gave him away to a loving home. He *was* a mutt. You love strays. They kill you with their need—"

Janet jumped in. "But BradKeanu was also the name of your company."

"I had a company?" I tossed my hair back, impressed with myself.

"A muff-making company," she explained, pulling a furry pink muff-purse from her backpack. "You manufactured these, but you couldn't meet the supply-demand thing so you had to shut down."

Amber interjected, "Because, excuse me, you had no clue how to actually run a company."

De shot her a silencing look.

Then Miss Geist and Mr. Hall told me how my efforts, on more than one occasion, had reminded them of their devotion. They claimed I was not only an excellent student, but like, such the matchmaker and proponent of rightful relationships. De and Murray dittoed.

Summer held up our school newspaper, but before she could contribute her memory, I was seized with a thought.

"I wrote for our school paper, didn't I?"

"Excellent!" Summer exclaimed, adding, "That was to meet a boy."

Annabelle started reciting lines from a play I recognized to be *Hamlet.*

"I was in that!" I yelled as I pictured a lacy handmaid's outfit.

Annabelle nodded. "That was also to meet a boy."

Murray produced a prototype for an exercise video, explaining, "You spearheaded the effort to get teenage America in shape. It almost panned out."

Suspiciously, I asked, "Was that also to meet a boy?"

De interjected, "In a way, but let's don't go there."

Suddenly, this vivid memory came fully back to me. Excitedly, I was all, "The Baldwin I was in love with. Tragically, he went off to war, didn't he? Just before he got mauled by a bear . . ." I trailed off.

Collectively, my t.b.'s and teachers groaned. "No,

Cher, that was *Legends of the Fall.* A movie. You didn't live it, you merely saw it," De clarified.

Abruptly, Amber stood up. "Excuse me, this is clearly not getting us anywhere. There must be some twelve-step memory rehab program she can join, like, Amnesiacs Anonymous. Or would they just call it Amnesiacs?"

Amber chortled at her bon mot, alone again, naturally.

Exasperated, Sean was all, "While it pains me to agree with Amber, this time, she's right. Cher's no closer to full memory recovery than she was when we started. Let's just bop her on the head again. That's how it worked when Lois Lane had amnesia on *Superman.*"

De took Sean up on his suggestion: with the rolled-up school newspaper, she bopped *him* on the head.

After school, I was giving De her props for the way extra-circular-y effort on my behalf, when her pager went off. As she checked the number, I guessed. "Your mom, again?"

"No, this time it's my boo. My mom and I are patched. She finally gave up stalking me."

"Did she ever say why she went volcanic at the concept of you going to the beach house?"

De exhaled. "Actually, Cher, she did. It took a while, but eventually we had this massively deep interface. I know you don't remember, but Miss Geist had nailed it. For some whack reason, my mom really was afraid of losing me. She was all, 'I know I sounded unreasonable, Dionne, but it suddenly hit me that you only have a few more years at home, and what if, after seeing your father, you decided to spend them with him? I'm not ready to let you go.'"

De continued, "So I was all, 'Hello, *mother?* And like, abandon my ferocious life in Beverly Hills? With you? As if! I'm totally the main star in your orbit. I'm copasetic with Dad, but among his clan, I'd be a mere supporting player in the soap opera of their fractious lives. And segue! Chandra doesn't even have the Chanel connection anymore. So, like, I need such tsuris? Not even. Besides, Mom—I totally love you.'

"Cher, you should have been there: it was such the *Full House* moment. We hugged, and instead of our usual air-kiss, made full mouth-to-cheek contact."

"De, I am beyond pumped that everything worked out for you."

"Only because of you, Cher."

"Tscha! I may have facilitated the journey, but you and your mom totally worked through your feelings on your own. Snaps to both of you, girlfriend!"

That night, Daddy was waxing nostalgic as he and I were flipping through the album of my baby pictures. When we came across a shot of toddler me playing with a baby turtle, he explained, "We bought it for you to commemorate your first two-syllable word. You pointed to one at the zoo and proudly said, 'tuh-tle.'"

Without thinking, I blurted, "Turtle? I always thought my first two-syllable word was AmEx."

Daddy's mouth flew open and his eyes grew wide. "That was always our family joke, Cher. You remembered!"

Oops, there it was again, a thought-fragment. I

tried to tease more out of it, but as suddenly as it had opened, the door to my back lot slammed shut.

I turned to him. "I wish I could remember more."

He hugged me. "You will, Cher. I'm sure of it." Only his voice betrayed his confidence.

That night, as I lay in bed unable to sleep, I thought about the photos Daddy and I had been sorting through. Suddenly, I was seized by the urge to check out that portrait of my mother. I threw on my XOXO chenille robe and matching slippers and silently slithered down stairs.

When I got to the bottom where the portrait hung—still off center a squinch—I stood there, gazing into her eyes as I tried to straighten it.

All at once, Mom seemed to be telling me something.

"'Zup, Mom? Can you unlock the secret of my memory?"

Something clicked. I don't know if Mom had the answer, but I fully believe she communicated to me, coaxing, "Hang in there, Cher. It won't be long."

I was trying to get her to be, like, more specific, when the sound of someone else shuffling down the steps startled me. I spun around, severely unthrilled at the specter of this interruption of my quality time with Mom.

But the sight of Josh, all rumpled hair and buttons askew on his pajama top, was beyond adorable. I felt the tiniest blush creep into my cheeks, so I went for casual. "Do you, like, live here full time now?"

Sleepy eyed, Josh shrugged. "Nah, but the food's better than at my dorm. I woke up and couldn't fall back to sleep, so I came downstairs for a snack."

As he disappeared into the kitchen, I called out, "Don't bother looking for the yogurt, you finished it . . ."

In a flash, Josh was back, wide awake. ". . . a few weeks ago. Cher, you remember that."

A rerun of Josh on the couch, scarfing the frozen frappaccino, had come to me. "You ate it right out of the container, right?"

"Cher, that's great! That's wonderful!"

In his glee, Josh threw his arms around me and pulled me close. I felt so safe. He ran his hands through my hair, and I tilted my head back to look at him. Our eyes locked.

"We're not related . . . like, in any way, DNA shape, or form, right?" I stammered.

Suddenly, Josh went all awkward and dropped his arms. "No, Cher, we're not. Different biological parents entirely. I'm, uh, gonna go hunt up . . . Maybe there's more yogurt in the fridge."

Josh turned away and headed back to the kitchen. Suddenly, it was like, thud. Right at that moment, I was fully angsting, awash in a despondency I had not allowed myself in the past two weeks. From what everyone had told me, I was such the optimist, and I didn't want to disappoint my public. But what if all the optimism was faux? What if I never got my memory back?

The air went out of me. Slowly, I sank down onto the cold, tiled floor at the bottom of the steps, right under Mom's portrait. My back pressed against the wall, I drew my knees up to my chest and hugged them tightly. I felt an errant tear stray down my cheek.

I didn't so much hear Josh come back as feel his presence as he quietly positioned himself on the floor next to me. He put his arm around me. With the other, he tilted my head toward his. Another tiny tear trickled down my cheek and Josh carefully traced its path with his finger. Then he put his hand at the base of my neck, in my hair. He moved his face closer to mine.

I closed my eyes. Ever so slowly, ever so softly, our lips met . . .

And that's when I heard it: *Thwack!*

And everything went black. Like, again.

Chapter 14

"Cher! Cher! Are you all right?"

"Call nine one one! Hurry up!"

Josh and Daddy were hovering over me, their faces ashen. As Josh fumbled with the phone on the marble pedestal by the stairs, Daddy bellowed, "How could you let this happen?"

Josh stammered into the phone, "I-I'd like to report—an emergency."

Without thinking, I bolted up and wrested the phone from him. "Hang on, Josh, I think I'm okay. Hold up on the nine one one."

Tentatively eyeing my dad, Josh allowed me to put the phone back in its cradle.

Daddy gripped my arm and tried to help me walk, but I waved him away. Rubbing my head, I began to circle the foyer slowly. I was feeling something fully miraculous, but I had to be sure it was real and that it wouldn't desert me after a few seconds.

With each turn around the hand-crafted ceramic-tiled floor, I felt surer. All the accessories began to look familiar. Correction: better than familiar. I knew this stuff; this stuff was mine!

I recognized the Chinese vases from the Ming dynasty, with their profusion of foliage from A Garden of Earthly Delights florists. I recognized the Matisse, the oil paintings, the Claes Oldenburg sculptures. I recognized social slug Josh in some hideous discount PJ getup, and my loving daddy in his Ralph Lauren silk jammies. I recognized the phone on the marble pedestal—and everything!

I took a deep breath and threw my arms around Daddy's neck. "I remember! I remember! Oh, Daddy, you're Mel, the fully prominent attorney! I'm Cher, your fully prominent daughter! This is our hacienda! This is our stuff!"

Daddy's jaw dropped as he stared at me, unbelieving. "Are you sure, Cher? Are you really sure? It's not just a little piece of memory this time—but the whole deal?"

Suddenly, my eye fell on the portrait of Mom. It was on the floor.

"What's Mom doing on the floor?" I asked.

Josh gulped. "The picture fell off the wall, Cher. You were sitting right under it. I tried to get you out of the way, but I wasn't fast enough. The corner of it hit you on the head."

That scene came back to me in a rush. That's when my jaw dropped. Mom's picture had dislodged and bopped me just as I was about to . . . *kiss* . . . the step-drone!

"Aaahhh!" I slapped my hands to my cheeks and let out a bloodcurdling scream. Had the producers of *Home Alone* been there, I would have been the new Macaulay Culkin.

I spent the next hour jogging down memory lane with Daddy, assuring him that I was furiously fine—I was chronic, I was golden, I was back!

Even Josh, after recovering from our near facial collision, helped by overruling Daddy's motion to get a doctor, just in case. Like in all due respect, I had had my fill of the medical profession.

Josh was all, "Watch, Mel, I'll prove she's her old self. Cher, snipe at me."

I totally grinned and fell happily into auto-snipe mode.

"Remind me again why you're here? Doesn't your dorm have grounds for abandonment? And those PJ's! Live in the now, Josh."

"At least I didn't have to max out my credit cards to get them, as I'm sure you did for that frilly, overpriced robe you've got on."

As Josh and I gleefully traded one-ups, I saw a tear slide down Daddy's cheek. Massively relieved, he threw his arms around both our shoulders, hugged us, and motioned toward the kitchen.

He was all, "My baby's back—finally. This calls for a celebration! Let's see if any I can use any of those high-falutin' kitchen gadgets to whip up some kind of trendo-ccino. Come on, kids. My treat. You two haven't seen anything until you've seen Mel Horowitz at the espresso machine."

Daddy started to lead us toward the kitchen, but I stopped short and twirled out from under his arm.

"I'll be right there," I said. "I have to do something first."

I waited until Daddy and Josh were fully out of sight. Then I picked up Mom's portrait from the floor and set her on the couch, where she'd be more comfortable until Daddy got the contractors—or whoever you called—to resecure her on the wall where she belonged.

I thought about the massive effort everyone around me had put in to my memory-rehab: Daddy, Josh, my t.b.'s, and my teachers, even the doctors and relatives. In their own way, they'd all contributed pieces of the puzzle. And by doing that, they'd shown me just how golden my life really was. It took my mom to, like, literally, knock them all into place. I suddenly remembered something Chad, that Sierra Club dude, had said: "It's about the journey, not the destination." It seemed to me that wasn't just about the road to Hana, but like, hello, life itself.

I pressed my fingers to my lips and then onto Mom's.

"Thanks, Mom. I knew I could count on you."

About the Author

Randi Reisfeld is the author of *Clueless: Too Hottie to Handle, Clueless: Cher Goes Enviro-Mental, Clueless: Cher's Furiously Fit Workout,* and *Clueless: An American Betty in Paris.* She has also authored *Who's Your Fave Rave? 40 Years of 16 Magazine* (Berkley, 1997) and *The Kerrigan Courage: Nancy's Story* (Ballantine, 1994), as well as several other works of young adult nonfiction and celebrity biographies. The *Clueless* series, duh, is totally the most chronic!

Ms. Reisfeld lives in the New York area with her family. And, grievously, the family dog.